SILENT NIGHT

A LANTERN BEACH CHRISTMAS NOVELLA

CHRISTY BARRITT

CASSIDY CHAMBERS

CASSIDY CHAMBERS LOWERED the crime report in her hands and stuffed it into a folder she'd soon hand over to temporary Lantern Beach Police Chief Braden Dillinger.

In two days, Christmas would be here, and crime in the Outer Banks was escalating. Stolen Christmas decorations, a store break-in, and even a couple of attempted kidnappings had occurred in recent weeks.

Not all those things happened on Lantern Beach, but the crime blotter covered the entire county. However, for the next three months, none of it would be Cassidy's problem.

Today, she was starting her maternity leave.

As she hiked her bag higher on her shoulder, she took one last glance around her office. Part of her would miss keeping an eye on her little community, but Dillinger had proven himself a capable officer. He would handle things while she was out. They'd already gone over all the details.

She rubbed her belly. Her very pregnant belly.

She couldn't wait for her baby to get here so she could experience the joys of motherhood. But she'd be lying if she denied she was nervous about the life change.

With a final glance back, she stepped into the reception area of the station. Dispatcher Paige Henderson smiled pleasantly from behind the front desk and pushed a basket her way.

"Someone left this outside for you, Chief Chambers."

"How nice." Cassidy stepped closer to examine the contents. Diapers. Wipes. A baby rattle. Some onesies.

The community had been so supportive, and on more than one occasion Cassidy had found packages on her doorstep—she'd even found one this morning. That wasn't to mention the fact that her church had given her a baby shower, as had the police department and several of her closest friends.

This new phase of her life was coming quickly, and Cassidy wasn't quite sure reality had kicked in. As police chief, she was used to sleepless nights and being responsible for others. But still . . . a baby.

Her baby.

She and Ty were finally going to be parents.

A grin feathered her lips.

She could hardly wait.

She plucked the card from the basket and read the words there.

So excited for your new delivery. Congrats!

"Who is it from?" Paige stared, her corkscrew curls bouncing as she leaned forward.

Cassidy showed her the card. "Someone who wants to remain anonymous, apparently."

"Well, that's very sweet that they left this."

"Yes, it is." Cassidy lifted the basket, resting it against her hip. "I'm heading home. I left everything for Officer Dillinger on my desk. He should be ready to go."

"Is Ty flying in tonight?"

Cassidy nodded. "His flight from Indianapolis keeps getting delayed because of bad weather. But he's hoping to catch one into Norfolk and then drive the rest of the way down."

"He's cutting it close, isn't he? Your baby is coming in two weeks—if not sooner."

"That's what he keeps saying, but I told him he should take this trip. It's important to Blackout that he gets this contract, and I'd rather him do it now then after our baby comes." Blackout was the private security firm Ty ran with his friend Colton Locke. It was based out of Lantern Beach, and the group's popularity had soared recently.

"You know we're here if you need us for anything." Paige flashed a smile. "Just let us know."

Gratitude filled Cassidy. The islanders had made it clear she was now officially one of them, even though she'd lived here only a few years.

With a nod goodbye to Paige, Cassidy stepped outside. The air felt brisk, especially now that the sun had set. The stars shone brightly overhead, and a sense of calm filled the air. Maybe she could get a little rest in before her baby came into this world.

Cassidy headed to her car. She'd already installed a baby seat in the back, just in case. Actually, Ty had insisted on doing so. He was going to be a doting father, there was no doubt about that.

She smiled at the thought.

Setting her basket on the car's hood, Cassidy pulled her purse toward her to retrieve her keys.

Sounds in the distance caught her ear.

She took a few tentative steps across the parking lot and glanced behind the station. A woman sat curled near the dumpster, an oversized coat covering her body and a scarf wrapped around her neck.

Concern rushed through Cassidy as she approached the woman. "Is everything okay?"

The woman looked up, her eyes bloodshot. "I'm

sorry. I didn't think anyone would hear me back here. I just need to take a rest for a moment."

Cassidy stepped closer. Something was off about this woman.

Her gaze traveled beyond the woman, and Cassidy spotted a dented car parked on the other side of the dumpster. Did that belong to the woman?

Cassidy looked back at the stranger. "Can I do anything for you?"

The woman used her sleeve to rub her wet eyes. "Something about this time of the year . . . it always makes me sad, you know? Other people have families to return home to, and I don't. It always hits me hard."

Cassidy's heart pounded with compassion. She hadn't seen her own family in nearly four years thanks to a hit that had been taken out on her life.

She shoved those thoughts aside. "I'm sorry to hear that. Are you in town to visit someone?"

"Yes, I'm actually trying to meet up with someone in particular." The woman's gaze met Cassidy's, and she pulled herself to her feet, wiping some dirt from her jacket as she heaved in a shaky breath. "I was just waiting for them to show up."

"Are they meeting you here?" Cassidy glanced around, looking for a sign of anyone else nearby.

"As a matter of fact, she is." Her gaze darkened. "But she doesn't know why I'm here yet."

"What?" This woman wasn't making any sense.

"I'm here for you, Cassidy. I wanted to find *you*."

Cassidy's instincts went on high alert, but before she could react, the woman charged toward her. Something slammed into her head.

Cassidy collapsed onto the ground. Her arms circled her belly, desperate to protect her baby.

Please, Lord, Cassidy prayed. *Protect my baby.*

Please.

But as the woman came at her again, everything went black.

2

TY CHAMBERS

TY DIALED Cassidy's number again. But, just as before, the call went straight to voice mail.

His jaw tightened as he shoved the phone back into his pocket. It wasn't like her not to answer, and he needed to give her a flight update.

He glanced around the airport at the other stranded passengers. So many people lingered in the terminal that there weren't enough available seats. Instead, travelers crowded the walkways. Some had set up camp in corners and nooks, trying to grab some shut-eye until the flights could be rescheduled. Some grumbled as if their discontent could miraculously change the weather. Others stared mindlessly at their phones.

Ty thought for sure he'd be able to catch the flight from Indianapolis to Norfolk before the weather caused delays. From there, he'd planned on driving down to Lantern Beach. It would make for a long travel day, but he was uncomfortable leaving Cassidy alone so close to her due date. With every moment that passed, he grew more uneasy.

Doc Clemson had said their baby could come any time in the next two weeks.

Cassidy had insisted he get this trip over with. So he had. He'd landed the contract, which meant they'd need to hire more guys for Blackout. Since there was a waiting list of experienced candidates eager for the opportunity, that wouldn't be a problem.

But now this trip seemed like a really bad idea.

He stared out the floor-to-ceiling windows that lined the airport wall. Snowdrifts blanketed the window ledges, and darkness stretched on the other side.

Ty didn't need sunlight to know snow covered everything out there. The unwelcome precipitation had thrown all the flight plans into a tailspin.

He sighed.

He took out his phone and tried Cassidy one more time, hoping she'd simply been caught up in some last-minute police work.

She still didn't answer.

That just wasn't like her.

She should have called back by now.

On a whim, he called his business partner and best friend, Colton Locke, who answered on the first ring.

"Hey, man," Colton said. "Did you make it home yet?"

Ty glanced out the window again. "Unfortunately, the weather has caused a lot of delays. I'm still working on trying to get a flight."

"I'm sorry to hear that. Tomorrow is Christmas Eve, so I hope it all works out. I'm sure everyone at that airport wants to get on the next available flight."

Ty scanned the crowds again and frowned. "You're right. They do."

"What's going on? You already told me about the meeting, so I assume you're not calling about that."

"Actually, I've been trying to get up with Cassidy, but I can't reach her. Could you check on her? It's just not like her to not answer. And with her being pregnant..."

"Of course. I'll do whatever I can. Do you know where she was going to be this evening?"

Ty glanced at his watch and saw that it was 8:30 p.m. already. "I know this was her last day in the office. I'll try the station next, but I'm afraid my phone is going to die. I already used my backup battery charger, and all the outlets at the airport are being used by other travelers right now. I didn't want my phone to completely die."

"Understood. I'll make some calls, ask around, and

get back with you. Maybe Cassidy just went out with her friends for some last-minute girl time before the baby comes."

Ty nodded. Colton's words made perfect sense. "As soon as you hear anything, let me know. Please."

"Of course. I'll call you back."

But as Ty put his phone away, a bad feeling lingered in his gut.

He had a feeling he would end up regretting this trip.

He prayed he was wrong.

3

COLTON LOCKE

AS SOON AS Colton Locke walked into the police station, he went straight toward Paige at the reception desk. He paused, his body tense as he turned to address her.

"I'm looking for Cassidy, and she's not answering her phone," he started, getting right to the point. "Have you seen her?"

"She left about thirty minutes ago to go home."

Colton's eyes narrowed. He didn't like the sound of that. "She didn't mention stopping anywhere else?"

"No, she said she planned to go home and wait for Ty." Paige paused and shoved her eyebrows together. "Why? What's going on?"

Colton straightened and let out a long breath, trying not to overreact—but overreacting wasn't something he was known for. His gut told him something could be wrong.

"Ty's been trying to get up with her, but Cassidy's not answering her phone."

Paige frowned. "That's unlike her."

"I know. I told Ty I would look for her. I wanted to start here."

"Do you want me to tell the other guys? Bradshaw is still on duty, and Dillinger will be here any minute. I'm sure they'd be happy to help."

He hoped it didn't come to that, that this was just a simple misunderstanding. But he couldn't say either way. Not yet. "Let me ask around more first, but I'll get back with you on that."

Colton stepped outside and crossed to the west side of the building. He hadn't seen Cassidy's car when he'd pulled up. But he needed to make sure she hadn't parked on the other side of the station.

He froze when he rounded the corner and spotted her sedan. A basket of baby items rested on the hood.

Cassidy had left that on her car?

Colton couldn't think of a single good reason she'd do that.

He reached for the gun holstered at his shoulder. As a former Navy SEAL and the co-director of the private security group Blackout, he felt like he was always at the ready. Sometimes, that paid off.

He prayed this wasn't one of those times.

Colton approached the vehicle. The doors were still locked. He checked the front and backseats and then glanced around, looking for a sign of what had happened.

Cassidy was nowhere in sight.

The scene in front of him didn't make sense.

Unless someone had picked Cassidy up and they'd gone somewhere together. Maybe Skye or Lisa, two of Cassidy's close friends, had swung by to surprise her with some last-minute fun.

But that still didn't explain the basket left on her car or why Cassidy wasn't answering her phone.

As Colton walked toward the back of the building, he paused.

A purse lay on the ground, contents from inside scattered around it.

He leaned down and picked up the cell phone lying there.

As he did, the screen lit. A picture of Cassidy and Ty filled it, along with notifications about several missed calls.

Colton's stomach dropped.

There was no way that Cassidy would have left her purse and phone out here—not unless something bad had happened.

He scooped up the items and rushed back into the police station.

Colton definitely needed some backup, especially if his initial conclusion was correct.

CASSIDY CHAMBERS

CASSIDY'S VISION FINALLY CLEARED.

As it did, she pushed herself up from the floor and blinked several times, trying to get a better idea of where she was.

She glanced around the bright white room with upholstery-paneled walls and frowned.

At once, everything flooded back to her.

The woman at the dumpster. Cassidy asking if she needed help. Feeling something hit her head.

Now this.

Cassidy's hand went to her protruding stomach. She frantically rubbed it, holding her breath until she felt her baby kick.

Her shoulders slumped as relief washed through her.

Her baby was okay.

Thank God.

But as Cassidy glanced at her belly, she noticed she was now wearing an oversized sweater and yoga pants.

These weren't her clothes.

Someone had changed her.

Her throat suddenly felt drier.

At once, she touched her arm and felt a tender spot near her bicep.

She'd been drugged, she realized. That's how this woman had gotten her here without Cassidy having any memories of it.

She rubbed her belly again, praying that whatever drug she'd been given wouldn't affect her precious baby.

Rage quickly joined forces with her worry. Rage like Cassidy had never felt before.

If someone thought they were going to get away with this . . . then they had another thing coming. Cassidy would make sure of it.

And if Cassidy didn't succeed, Ty would. She had no doubt about that.

She glanced around again, trying to figure out how to escape.

The room was only about eight by eight with carpet on the floor beneath her. There were no windows, only a white interior door in front of her with a small doorknob.

And there was the silence. She'd heard the expression "deafening silence" before. But she'd never experienced it until now. She couldn't hear anything—no birds or people talking or even the wind blowing.

The realization left her feeling unnerved.

She tried to push herself to her feet but wobbled.

Instead, she sank back to the floor. She couldn't risk falling.

She attempted to draw in a deep breath, but breathing was already more difficult now that the baby pressed on her lungs. Add anxiety to that, and the task nearly felt impossible.

Instead, Cassidy tried to gather her strength. She just needed a few more minutes. Then she would try to get up again.

At once, a lullaby began playing in the room.

She glanced up and saw a single speaker and a camera mounted in the corner ceiling across from her.

Cassidy's heart beat harder.

Someone was watching her right now.

Disgust churned inside her.

She managed to stand and waddled toward the camera, staring at the lens dead center. "Hey! What do you think you're doing? Let me out of here!"

Cassidy knew her demands wouldn't do any good. But she needed to let the woman who'd done this to her know she wasn't just going to accept this fate.

She pounded on the walls, trying to make as much noise as possible.

A moment later, the music stopped, and a voice cut through the room. "I wouldn't waste my energy if I were you. You're in a soundproof room. No one is going to hear you. No one but me . . . and your baby. I'd hate it if you upset him or her."

A sickly feeling gurgled in Cassidy's stomach.

Just what was this woman planning on doing?

Cassidy remembered their conversation before she'd blacked out.

I'm trying to meet up with someone in particular . . . but she doesn't know why I'm here yet . . .

An inkling of the truth tried to whisper into her consciousness.

But Cassidy wasn't ready to face the truth. Not yet.

Instead, she rubbed her belly again.

No one was going to hurt her baby, she vowed.

No one.

BRADEN DILLINGER

ACTING POLICE CHIEF Braden Dillinger turned toward Colton Locke, Officer Dane Bradshaw, Officer Jonathan Banks, and Austin Brooks—one of Ty's best friends. They all met in the conference room at the police station after being alerted about Cassidy's disappearance.

"I sent an all-points bulletin throughout this county and the surrounding ones," Braden started.

"Smart thinking," Colton muttered as he stood rigidly near the door.

"I also contacted the transportation system about shutting down the ferries. The Coast Guard will be on the lookout for any boats in the area. The waters are rough right now because of the wind, so they doubt anyone in their right mind will try to leave the island."

"That's good news." Bradshaw rubbed his jaw as he

also stood—in fact, no one seemed comfortable enough to sit, not when the situation felt so urgent. "If someone grabbed Cassidy, we *can't* let them get off this island. Our chances of finding her are much better here on Lantern Beach."

There were no bridges leading to the island, so only ferries and boats were available for transportation. But Braden was glad the weather was actually working in their favor right now.

"What's next?" Banks asked. "We've got to find Cassidy."

Talk about being thrown into the fire . . . Braden hadn't even made it in for his first shift when he'd gotten this call.

And it was one he'd never wanted to receive. Ty and Cassidy were two of his closest friends. Braden's wife, Lisa, was Cassidy's best friend. He hadn't broken the news to Lisa yet about what was going on. He'd need to tell her soon. The last thing he wanted was for Lisa to hear about this from someone besides him.

Braden glanced at the list in front of him. "We need to put together search parties and go house by house throughout the island. The more groups we have out there looking for her, the better."

"My team and I can put together the search parties." Colton stepped forward. "I'll head them up for you."

"That sounds great." Braden glanced at the notebook where he was taking notes.

"I'll check security footage from the front of the station and nearby businesses to see if the cameras picked up anything," Banks said. "I can do that while you guys get the search parties organized."

"I'll call in Mac also," Braden said. Mac MacArthur was the island's former police chief and one of Cassidy's closest friends. "Ty will want Mac to know so he can help. Has anyone called Ty with the update?"

Colton rubbed his jaw and frowned. "I did—probably the hardest call I've had to make in a long time."

"Is he able to get back soon?" Braden couldn't imagine what his friend was going through.

Colton shook his head, the lines on his forehead deepening. "All flights are grounded out of Indianapolis right now. He can try to drive back, but it's going to be at least sixteen hours if he does."

"What about Ranger?" Banks glanced at Bradshaw. "Could we send him out there to try to track down Cassidy's scent?"

Ranger was Bradshaw's police dog, a boxer mix, who'd proven valuable on more than one occasion.

Bradshaw frowned and shook his head. "I wish we could. But the wind is strong tonight, so I doubt there's a trail left. I wish that wasn't true but . . ."

"Has anyone been to Ty and Cassidy's house yet?"

Austin asked. Braden had called him to ask if he'd seen Cassidy, and Austin had come right to the station.

"Not yet," Braden said. "Why don't you do that for us?"

It seemed like a safe enough assignment for his non-law enforcement friend.

Austin stepped toward the door as if anxious to do his job. "I will. Then I'll be back here to help with the search. If I find anything at the house, I'll let you know right away."

"Thanks."

With everyone's assignments doled out, Braden grabbed his phone to call Mac. He'd tried him earlier, but Mac hadn't answered. If he remembered correctly, Mac was heading to the gun range at the Blackout headquarters today. He probably had noise-blocking earmuffs on and couldn't hear his cell phone. When he didn't answer again, Braden left a message, asking him to call ASAP.

They needed to get busy.

Because it wasn't bad enough that their friend and police chief was missing.

The fact that Cassidy was pregnant and close to delivery only added more urgency to this situation.

6

AUSTIN BROOKS

AUSTIN CLIMBED the steps to Ty and Cassidy Chambers' home. The oceanfront cottage was charming and rustic with a great view of the Atlantic. Their Bible study group had spent many evenings having beach bonfires, playing volleyball, and sharing about their lives on those sandy shores.

Austin knocked at the front door, not expecting an answer.

As he waited, something pounced on the glass panes atop the door.

He drew back, bracing himself for trouble.

Then he realized it was Kujo.

Just Kujo.

Austin almost laughed—although this wasn't a laughing situation.

Despite his scary name, the golden retriever was a teddy bear.

He'd spotted Austin, and the dog's tail was already wagging.

Someone needed to let the dog out since Cassidy and Ty weren't home. Austin would do that while he was here.

He tried the door handle, but, as he suspected, it was locked.

He pulled an extra key from his pocket. He'd done some construction work here in the past, as well as acted as house sitter, so he had one of Ty's spares. He'd never enter Cassidy and Ty's home without their permission unless it was an emergency.

This seemed like an emergency.

A moment later, Austin pushed the door open.

As Kujo greeted him with a tail wag and quick sniff, Austin glanced around the house. Everything appeared to be in place, all the way down to the throw blankets and pillows on the couch. A Christmas tree stood in the corner, cheerfully decorated. Garland had been strung across the mantle. A nativity scene sat on the coffee table.

There were no signs that Cassidy had come here after work.

Just to be certain, Austin decided to check the rest of the place.

He let Kujo spend some time outside while he

looked through the house.

He paused at one of the spare bedrooms and peered inside. A crib had been set up, along with a changing table and dresser. A rocking chair sat in one corner, and a white rug stretched across the floor.

A pang of sorrow pounded through him.

Cassidy should be getting ready to enjoy her baby. But now someone had interrupted her life, and he couldn't imagine why.

Unless someone was trying to get revenge on Cassidy for putting them away for a crime. Could a member of Gilead's Cove have returned to the island to hurt her?

When Cassidy had broken up the cult, many members were furious with her.

Or what about that high-profile case she'd worked last year involving the senator?

Or did this go back to Ty and his work as a SEAL? He'd helped put his fair share of bad guys away.

Austin didn't have enough information to know the answers.

He paused in the kitchen and stared at a basket on the kitchen counter. Self-care items were inside— prenatal vitamins, a foot mask, some scented lotion. The note—displayed on the front—read, "Take good care of yourself."

Austin leaned in closer as he studied the yellow bow on the front.

Was that . . . ?

He plucked something from the center of the bow and sucked in a breath.

A small camera had been mounted at the center of the bow. If he hadn't been on edge tonight as he searched for Cassidy, he probably wouldn't have ever noticed.

Had someone been spying on Cassidy?

The bad feeling in his gut grew even stronger.

Austin called Ty's number. He didn't want to overwhelm his friend with too many phone calls right now, but Ty needed to know about this.

"Anything?" Ty answered on the first ring.

"I'm at your house. No signs of Cassidy. You know anything about a gift with spa-like items sitting on the kitchen counter?"

"Can't say I do. Why?"

Austin explained about the small camera.

"I don't like the sound of that." Ty's voice sounded tight with worry.

"I don't either. I'll make sure to feed Kujo before I leave, and then I'll let the rest of the guys know what I found."

"Do that. Please. I'm afraid something terrible has happened to Cassidy."

A lump formed in Austin's throat. "We're going to find her. I promise you, we're doing everything we can."

7

CASSIDY CHAMBERS

CASSIDY HAD YELLED until her throat hurt—but to no avail. Finally, she collapsed against the wall, feeling her blood pressure rising and whooshing in her ears.

As she tried to steady her breathing, she stared at the door.

What the woman had said over the intercom was probably true. This room appeared to be soundproof.

That fact didn't help Cassidy figure out where she was, however.

What kind of person had a soundproof room in their home?

Not anyone she knew.

What if she wasn't in a home at all? What if she was in some kind of facility?

Cassidy wasn't sure how long she'd been knocked out or what time it was. Could she have been unconscious long enough for this woman to have taken her off Lantern Beach?

She frowned at the thought as unknowns haunted her, nagged her, tried to promise despair.

Concentrate on the concrete, on what you do know.

Cassidy swallowed hard and tried to focus her thoughts.

What did she know?

She squeezed her eyes shut. If she remembered correctly, forecasters had warned of rough seas. Knowing that, she found it hard to believe that she'd been taken off Lantern Beach.

The soundproof room? It wasn't even a safe room, not if Cassidy had to guess. The door didn't look high security. It didn't match what she knew about those rooms. There also didn't seem to be any provisions set up —like an emergency phone or food and water supplies.

As a pang ripped through her abdomen, the breath left her lungs.

Was this a contraction?

Panic tried to well inside her, but Cassidy shoved it down.

This was *not* a labor pain. She'd just gone to see Doc Clemson yesterday, and he'd said her pregnancy was on track—she still had two weeks to go.

But what if the stress of this situation had thrown Cassidy into early labor?

Cassidy's heart sped even faster, but she tried to keep it under control.

Panicking will only make the situation worse. Might even harm your child. You've got to manage it, Cassidy.

She took several deep breaths until she felt her heart rate slow.

The pang passed.

Thank You, Jesus.

But she couldn't be certain the pain wouldn't come again.

Cassidy scanned the room one more time. How was she going to get out of here?

She had to exhaust every possibility. At this point, she had no other choice.

Gathering her strength, she forced herself to crawl across the floor. She paused in front of the door and gripped the doorknob. As she suspected, the door was locked solid.

She sank back down.

There was nothing else in the room. Nothing to look inside or explore or use as a weapon.

She had no food or drink. No place to sit. No blanket to keep warm. No place to even go to the bathroom.

Cassidy pressed her eyes closed and began praying, trying to fight the despair growing inside her.

You've gone through other seemingly impossible situa-

tions. You can get through this one too. Just keep a calm, cool head.

But since becoming pregnant, her emotions had been stronger than ever. Cassidy normally prided herself in being levelheaded. But hormones had done something to her recently. All her emotions felt more vivid, and she could cry at the drop of a hat.

That wasn't a labor pain. It was probably a Braxton Hicks contraction. A false alarm.

Cassidy nodded. That had to be it.

Just a false alarm.

With any luck, she wouldn't feel any more contractions for a long time—preferably not until she was out of this place and safe with Ty.

As a noise sounded at the door, her breath caught.

She scooted away as it opened.

A woman holding a gun and a paper bag stepped into the room.

It was the woman from near the dumpster.

The one who'd knocked her out.

Anger flared to life inside Cassidy.

She wanted to lunge at her. To fight her.

But that woman had a gun and Cassidy didn't.

The woman closed the door behind her, her eyes glimmering with apparent excitement as she observed Cassidy. All signs of distress were gone. Clearly, that had been a manipulation tactic.

Now that Cassidy could see the woman better in

the light, she observed her captor's squarish face. Her short, unflattering hairstyle. Her stout build and over-sized T-shirt and baggy jeans.

"Oh, good . . . you're awake." The woman stared down at Cassidy and frowned with supposed compassion. "I'm sorry I had to get you here like that. I didn't have many options."

"Why are you doing this?" Cassidy folded her arms over her abdomen, desperate to protect her baby.

More than anything, she wanted to pull herself to her feet. To charge the woman and knock her to the ground. To fight until she gained her freedom.

But Cassidy couldn't take the chance of a stray bullet flying—and she also didn't have the energy to use her self-defense skills to get out of this. She felt so weak, probably a side effect of the sedative she'd been given.

"Everything is going to be okay." Her captor's voice took on a sickly, almost nurturing tone as she gazed down at Cassidy. "Trust me."

Cassidy trusted this woman just about as much as she trusted a druggie desperate for another hit.

The woman tossed the paper bag toward Cassidy. "You need to eat. The baby needs nourishment."

The way the woman said the words—as if she were intimately aware of Cassidy's needs—made the sick feeling in Cassidy's stomach grow even more intense.

Cautiously, Cassidy opened the bag. A bottle of water and sandwich rested inside.

Her stomach grumbled at the sight of it. How could she be hungry at a time like this? Then again, her cravings had been out of control lately.

Still, Cassidy wouldn't give this woman the satisfaction of doing what she said. She threw the bag down instead.

"I don't want to eat," Cassidy announced. "I want you to let me go. You do know who I am, don't you? The police chief? People are going to be out there searching for me."

The woman grinned, not even a hint of fear in her gaze. "But no one's going to find you. That's the beautiful part about this. They won't be able to hear you cry out. They could be in the next room and still not hear you. In fact, you could go into labor and yell and scream, and no one would be the wiser for it."

The sick feeling in Cassidy's stomach grew stronger.

This woman appeared to have thought about everything.

And Cassidy didn't know how to defend herself while protecting her baby.

MAC MACARTHUR

FORMER POLICE CHIEF Mac MacArthur rushed to the police station as soon as he got the call about what was going on.

He considered Cassidy the daughter he'd never had. She called him her mentor, but Mac had learned just as much from Cassidy as she had from him.

When he thought about both Cassidy and her precious baby being in danger, anger surged through him. He couldn't even begin to imagine how Ty must be feeling not being here to search for Cassidy. He prayed Ty would be able to get here soon.

As Mac walked up to the police station, he nearly collided with Colton Locke.

"Mac." Colton paused. "I'm glad you're here."

"Any updates?"

Colton's jaw tightened as he shook his head. "Not

yet, but we're still hopeful. Part of my team is already out there scouring the island. Another team is about to go out."

"Let me know what you find out. I'm going to do some good old-fashioned police work," Mac said. "I'll see what I can turn up."

"You do that. Keep us updated as well. Please."

Mac promised he would and then stepped around the side of the building to check out the area where the purse was found.

He paused and glanced around, wondering if there was anything the others had missed.

No security cameras faced this side of the building, and if Cassidy had been abducted near the dumpster, which Mac suspected was the case, then there would be little evidence to go on. But there had to be some way to find out more information.

The cold weather had probably kept most people in their homes this evening. The wind was downright chilly, and there wasn't much to do on the island past dark in the winter. That decreased their chances of having any witnesses.

Mac's gaze stopped on a house across the street.

Tim and Jan Stephens lived there. They were long-time island residents, and Mac knew them fairly well. Maybe they had seen something.

He strode across the street and paused by their front door.

A video doorbell had been mounted there.

Mac's pulse quickened.

He rang the bell and waited until they answered.

A few minutes later, the three of them gathered around the dining room table, Tim's phone in front of them. He found video footage from an hour ago and hit Play.

Mac's breath caught as he watched Cassidy approach a woman who lay curled in a ball against the dumpster. No doubt Cassidy had been trying to help someone in distress. Cassidy was a protector. Helping people is what she did.

Had someone exploited that fact?

After talking for a few minutes, the woman stood and withdrew something from her pocket.

The next instant, Cassidy fell to the ground.

Anger blazed through Mac.

That woman had hit Cassidy over the head with something.

She'd hit a pregnant woman.

Disgusted, Mac continued to watch as the woman pulled out a syringe, stabbed Cassidy in the arm and then dragged Cassidy across the gravel lot to a car parked just beyond the dumpster.

As the vehicle drove off, Mac squinted as he tried to get a better look at the license plate.

But the video was too dark, too grainy to make out any details.

Maybe he could enlarge the image on a different computer.

It was worth a try.

At least they now knew they were looking for a burly, twenty-something woman with dark hair.

It was something.

But Mac knew it wasn't enough.

ROCCO FOSTER

BLACKOUT OPERATIVE ROCCO FOSTER felt the tension growing between his shoulders as he ended his call with Colton. Rocco had been helping Peyton, his girlfriend, at her bakery when he'd heard his cell phone ring.

Peyton had thrown a Christmas party for some local elementary kids who'd won a baking contest. The night had been festive with happy Christmas music playing, lots of sugar cookies being decorated, and the smell of warm apple cider floating in the air.

But after Rocco learned what had happened to Cassidy, he knew he couldn't stay.

Instead, he explained to Peyton what had happened before heading back to headquarters to pick up Benjamin James, another member of Blackout.

Once he had Benjamin in the car, the two of them helped search the island for Cassidy.

Thanks to Mac MacArthur, they had a basic description of the vehicle linked with Cassidy's abduction. Rocco would search this island all night until he found that car if that's what he had to do.

He promised himself that.

Cassidy Chambers was one of the most likable people he'd ever met. Not only that, but she was also as tough as nails. No one dared walk on her.

That's what made this even harder. That and the fact that his friend and boss, Ty, was wrapped up in this.

Rocco and Benjamin cruised the dark streets of Lantern Beach, keeping their eyes open for the dark-green sedan. They would wake up people in the middle of the night if they had to. Anything to find that vehicle. It had to be somewhere in Lantern Beach. With the ferry closed, there would be no way to get a car off this island.

They had driven down the main road to the end. Now, as they headed back, they would hit each of the side streets.

Ten streets later, Rocco and Benjamin had seen a lot of Christmas decorations, including string lights and yard inflatables that swayed with the wind. But no green sedan.

He didn't want to feel discouraged, but time was of the essence right now.

"What's that?" Benjamin pointed to something glinting in the headlights.

"Let's find out." Rocco pulled to the side of the road and climbed from his SUV.

His breath caught as he stepped closer.

A car had been hidden in the brush.

And the vehicle matched the description of the one they were looking for.

As Benjamin called Colton to tell him the update, Rocco pulled on a glove and opened the unlocked door, hoping to find some evidence inside.

The first thing he spotted in the backseat was an empty syringe.

His breath caught.

This wasn't the news he'd been hoping for.

Now, it was even more urgent to find Cassidy.

The only good news was that maybe they could get a print off the syringe or a hit on who owned this vehicle.

10

CASSIDY CHAMBERS

CASSIDY STARED at the woman in front of her, knowing she needed to find out more about her adversary if she wanted to figure out a way to escape.

"What's your name?" Cassidy finally asked.

"Why do you want to know?" The woman's voice took on a defensive edge as she glared at Cassidy. She still stood with gun in hand, towering over Cassidy.

Cassidy swallowed hard. "I'd like to call you by your name. I'm Cassidy."

"I know who you are," the woman snapped. "I've been watching you the past couple of days."

Had Cassidy really been so distracted with this pregnancy that she hadn't noticed that? Regret instantly filled her.

She should have been more on guard. She usually prided herself on being observant.

But Cassidy knew she hadn't been at the top of her game lately. Her back ached too much. Her swollen ankles made it hard to walk. Her lungs often felt squeezed and tight.

The woman sneered. "If you have to know, my name is Jenn."

Cassidy leaned against the wall, trying to look entirely more casual than she felt. "Why do you have me here, Jenn?"

"Why are you asking so many questions?" The woman flung her hand through the air as if to emphasize her point, moving entirely too flippantly with a weapon in hand. "I came here to bring you something to eat. You need to stay healthy for the baby."

Cassidy nodded slowly, not wanting Jenn to have any type of knee-jerk reaction and accidentally pull the trigger. "I'll eat."

Jenn's shoulders slumped as if Cassidy's words had calmed her. "Good. I don't want to risk anything happening to you."

Cassidy let out a breath. Maybe that was a good sign. Jenn didn't want anything to happen to Cassidy . . . yet. But a clearer picture had formed in Cassidy's mind.

The attempted kidnappings Cassidy had read about earlier today . . . they'd involved infants.

What if this woman was somehow connected?

It only made sense.

"How many more days until you're due?" Jenn continued to stare at Cassidy, the unsteadiness growing in her gaze.

This woman wasn't quite right, wasn't quite in touch with reality. Her glazed eyes, stiff words, and flippant actions made that clear.

"Two weeks." Cassidy rubbed her belly again.

"Two weeks? I didn't think you had that much time left." Jenn's lips twisted as if the information threw her off guard and she needed to recalculate.

Cassidy protectively wrapped her arms over her belly, wanting to shield her baby from whatever was coming. That was her job—to protect her child.

What if she failed?

As a cry caught in her throat, she shoved the thought aside.

You can't think like that. You're going to figure out a way out of this. You defeated the deadly gang DH-7. You can defeat this woman too.

"I'm just telling you what the doctor said," Cassidy told her, careful to keep her voice calm and even.

"Two weeks? You're huge. I thought you were farther along." Jenn began pacing the small space, gun still in her hand. "How can I keep you here for two weeks? I'm going to have to get more food. More supplies."

Cassidy swallowed hard at the thought of staying in

this room for two weeks. "You don't have to keep me here at all."

Jenn turned toward Cassidy, rage flaring to life in her gaze. "Yes, I do! I've come this far. Do you even realize how hard it was to get you up here?"

Up here? So, she wasn't on ground level, which indicated she was still at the beach. Most of the homes here were built on stilts.

"Up where?" Maybe if Cassidy had a better idea where she was, she could form a plan on how to escape ... The more information she could gather, the better.

"It's not important. The only thing you need to know is that no one will find you. I covered all my tracks just to make sure. Nothing is going to get in the way between me and the baby. Do you understand?" Each word was said through clenched teeth. Jenn's nostrils even flared as she glared down at Cassidy.

Nausea gurgled inside Cassidy. This woman couldn't be reasoned with. Her mind wouldn't be changed.

Cassidy would need to figure out a Plan B.

"I understand," Cassidy murmured.

It was just as she feared.

This woman wanted her baby.

And as soon as she gave birth, Jenn was going to kill Cassidy.

11

LISA DILLINGER

LISA DILLINGER LOOKED up as the front door to her small apartment opened.

Braden, her husband, stepped inside.

She let out a breath when she spotted him. Being around Braden always made her feel better. Ever since they'd met, she'd known the two of them were a perfect match, and she thanked God every day for bringing him into her life.

But when Lisa noticed the worried expression on his face, any sense of peace disappeared.

She closed the door to the room of their fourteen-month-old daughter, Julia. The active toddler had finally gone down for bed—but only after putting up a fight.

Lisa slowly—cautiously—walked toward Braden, sensing he had bad news.

He planted a kiss on her cheek before studying her a moment. "Are you okay?"

"I'm fine." Lisa nodded, anxious to hear what he was about to say. "What's going on?"

He glanced at Julia's door before taking Lisa's hand and leading her into their bedroom. Lately, they both walked on eggshells, fearing waking their daughter up. She'd been a terrible sleeper—and a bit of a tyrant. But, still, she was the sweetest little tyrant Lisa had ever known.

"It's Cassidy . . ." Braden's voice cracked as he stood in front of her.

"Cassidy?" Lisa's heart jumped into her throat. "What happened? Is it the baby? Did she go into labor early? She's thirty-eight weeks, which means the baby can usually be born without issue—"

Braden shook his head, stopping her thoughts. "Cassidy is missing."

Lisa gasped, unsure if she'd heard him correctly. "What do you mean *missing*?"

"She left the police station this evening to start her maternity leave, and she never made it home. We found her car and purse still at the station, and no one's heard from her."

Lisa's thoughts raced through her in a frenzy of questions. "Have you tried calling?"

He shook his head somberly. "Her phone was with her bag."

"When did she leave the station? It had to only be a couple of hours ago, right? She couldn't be but so far . . ."

Braden's hand clamped her bicep, and he squeezed as of trying to reassure her. "Everyone's searching the island for her."

"Braden . . ." Lisa didn't even know what else to say. What *was* there to say? The thought of something happening to Cassidy at nine months pregnant . . . it was horrifying. "Are there any leads?"

"We found the car the woman who abducted her used. Unfortunately, it was stolen. We're trying to run prints, but there's nothing yet."

Her frown deepened. "I want to get out there and help look."

Braden's lips pulled into a taut line. "The best thing you can do right now is to stay here with Julia."

Lisa started to argue, but she knew that Braden was right. She needed to be with her child.

Braden's hand covered her belly. "Plus, I need to know you're safe."

Lisa's hand covered his. "Do you think someone's targeting pregnant women?"

"I don't know. But it's a theory."

She frowned. "But no one knows we're pregnant. Not yet. I want to make it to three months before I tell anyone."

"I know. I'm glad you talked me out of it because I

wanted to tell everyone. Now . . . that seems like a terrible idea."

Braden had been so excited he'd been ready to shout it from the rooftops. The memory warmed Lisa's heart. He was such a great dad.

She reached up and touched the side of his face where lines of worry had appeared. "I'll stay here with Julia. I promise."

He gave her a quick kiss before stepping back. "I need to keep searching. But I wanted to give you the news. I didn't want you to hear it from anyone else."

"I appreciate it."

"I know this is a longshot but . . ." He pulled out his phone and showed her a grainy picture. "You ever seen this woman?"

As Lisa studied the image, her breath caught. "As a matter fact, I have. She was in The Crazy Chefette yesterday."

Braden's eyes lit with excitement. "You're sure?"

"Positive."

"Did she pay with a credit card?"

Lisa tried to rewind her thoughts. "I don't remember, but I can check."

"If we can find out her name, that would be a huge help. Do you remember anything else about her?"

Lisa searched her memories for anything that had stood out about the woman.

That's when she realized there had been something significant.

Her stomach sank as fear tried to grip her.

Braden squeezed her arm. "What is it, Lisa?"

"There was a family with a baby eating at the restaurant," Lisa said. "This woman stopped by their table to tell them how beautiful their daughter was. Something seemed off about the woman, but I didn't think much of it at the time."

Braden frowned. "Let's see if we can find that receipt. We don't have any time to waste."

12
____

TY CHAMBERS

THE HELPLESSNESS BUILDING inside Ty made him want to jump out of his skin.

He was next in line to talk to someone about reserving a rental car. He'd wanted to leap to the front, but he'd waited his turn.

All flights were still grounded.

He *had* to figure out something else.

It looked like he needed to call in some favors.

If he could drive south for about two hours to where the weather wasn't this bad, he might be able to charter a private plane to get back to Lantern Beach. It was a longshot, but it was the only thing he could think of.

First, he needed to secure a car.

There had only been a few times in his life he'd felt

this powerless. And he hated it. Hated being stuck here when his wife needed him.

He should have never taken this trip.

But it was too late to change that now.

Right now, all Ty wanted was to get back to Lantern Beach.

Colton had been calling with updates, but none of them had been encouraging.

A woman had hit Cassidy over the head and knocked her out . . . and then drugged her.

Ty's stomach churned at the thought.

What if that drug affected their baby somehow? That wasn't even to mention Cassidy and what she must be enduring . . .

He took a few deep breaths, trying to calm himself.

Cassidy was extremely capable. But she still must be terrified. Being pregnant had brought out a new side of her, a more vulnerable one. That also meant she was at a disadvantage. She couldn't defend herself as she normally would.

As the person in front of him moved, Ty stepped forward to talk to the woman at the front desk. He prayed this plan would work . . . because he didn't have many options right now.

13

REBECCA MARKS

"TELL me again exactly what you need." Realtor Rebecca Marks stood beside her husband, Levi, as they stared at Colton Locke, who'd come to their front door.

She'd met the man a couple of times in the past, but she didn't know him well. Mostly, she knew of him as being Ty Chambers' friend.

But anyone coming to her door past nine at night made her cautious. She'd been getting ready for bed when she'd heard the doorbell ring.

Thankfully, Levi was here.

"Come in for a moment." Levi stepped back so Colton could get out of the cold.

Colton paused in the doorway, and his gaze went to Rebecca. "It's my understanding that your rental company is one of only a handful on the island that rents houses during the winter season. I need a list of everyone who's renting a house right now, and the addresses. Could you get that for me? Please?"

Colton explained the situation to them, and Rebecca's heart rate doubled at the thought of what Cassidy might be going through.

Normally, she wouldn't share her customers' private information. But in this case, she had no choice.

"Come on in." She nodded, indicating for Colton to follow her. "I'll see what I can find out. But I just put Emma down so we should keep our voices low."

"Of course."

As she went into the dining room, where she had a desk set up in the corner, Levi and Colton chatted. Her husband had worked for Homeland Security, so of course he would be concerned with a matter like this.

Her hands trembled as she pulled up the rental information. She hoped she might find something that helped. While it was true that her management company was one of the few still operating at this time of the year, there were also private rentals she wouldn't be able to get listings for.

Despite that, she printed off the list of renters and handed it to Colton. "I hope this helps. I truly do."

He glanced at the information and scanned the names. "We do too. We're trying to go house by house.

But time is of the essence right now, given Cassidy's condition."

Rebecca frowned. "I can imagine. I'll try to put in a call with a few other people I know who have rental houses. I'll see if they have anyone using them this week, if that helps."

"Any information you can give us would help." Colton glanced at the list again. "Is there any way to verify these people's identities? Did they have to show you a driver's license or anything when they checked in?"

"We generally take their credit card information."

"But somebody could use a prepaid debit card, right?"

Rebecca frowned. "I suppose they could do that if they had enough money on it. I can pull up the footage from the rental office. I've done that for Cassidy a couple times when she was looking for somebody. Would that help if you saw her face?"

"Absolutely. I'll send you a picture of this woman." Colton glanced at Levi. "In the meantime, I need to continue searching. Is there any way you could go over the footage and see if you recognize anyone who looks like this?"

"Anything we can do to help," Levi said. "Send a copy of the photo to my phone too."

"I will. Please let me know the moment you find out anything."

Rebecca wrapped her arms across her chest and lifted a prayer that Cassidy would be okay. Or the most wonderful time of the year might turn into a real-life nightmare.

14

CASSIDY CHAMBERS

JENN SAT across the room from Cassidy watching her eat. She'd insisted she wouldn't leave until every last bite was gone.

Cassidy's gaze remained on the door leading into the room. Jenn hadn't closed it all the way—it was still cracked open about an inch.

Was this Cassidy's chance to escape?

That thought kept replaying in her mind.

Cautiously, Cassidy lifted the top piece of bread from her sandwich. She wanted to make sure nothing was on the sandwich she shouldn't eat.

The hot ham with melted cheese looked normal. But why bother to heat it up? Did the woman know it was recommended that deli meat be heated to kill any bacteria before a pregnant woman consumed it?

Maybe she was reading too much into this.

Either way Cassidy prayed this food was safe for her baby.

Cassidy couldn't stay here for two weeks until her baby was born. She wouldn't let this woman take her baby away from her.

It was *not* going to happen.

As Jenn watched, Cassidy nibbled on the bread. Nausea continued to turn in her stomach, hinting that she could throw up at any minute.

She swallowed the cry rising in her throat and tried to take another bite of her sandwich. Everything had a bland, almost sour taste to it.

But she had to try to eat. If Cassidy could just regain some strength, then maybe she could figure out a way to escape.

She leaned against the wall and raised her sandwich but hesitated before taking another bite as the scent made her gag. If she ate more of this, she was going to throw up. She was certain of it.

"You need to eat," Jenn barked through clenched teeth. "The baby needs food."

"I'm trying. But my stomach doesn't feel right. What did you give me?"

"Nothing that would hurt my baby. I checked first. That's all you need to know."

My baby? Cassidy's heart pounded harder.

"Why are you doing this?" Cassidy decided to try the question again. If she could get inside this woman's mind, maybe that would help her devise a plan.

"All I want is a baby to love, and who will love me back. Being a mom is all I've thought about for years. I tried to find a husband, but no one seemed interested. So, I finally decided I was tired of waiting for a man to come along and give me what I wanted. I decided to get a baby no matter what it takes. When I saw you, I knew you'd be perfect."

"Why me?"

"Because you're pretty and looked so happy. Your baby will probably be pretty and happy also. I'm going to have a life like yours." Jenn grinned, even though her gaze looked distant and out of touch with reality. "My life is going to be perfect. I'll have everything I ever wanted."

The nausea in Cassidy's stomach churned harder. "Did you try to steal other babies in the Outer Banks before you kidnapped me?"

Jenn's gaze darkened. "I didn't try to *steal* them. I tried to rescue them. No one can love a baby like I can. I can give them a *better* home. A better life."

"Where is this better home going to be? Do you already have a nursery set up? Did you buy food to feed the baby? Diapers? Do you earn enough money to support a child?"

Jenn raised her chin, almost defiantly. "As a matter fact, I do. I have an apartment with all the baby stuff I need. I told my neighbors I was adopting a baby. Some of them have already given me some cute little outfits. They won't be asking any questions. I have all the details worked out."

Had this woman suffered from some type of psychotic break? It was the only thing that made sense. No rational person would come up with a plan like this.

And if Jenn had a break, would the psychosis subside? Would the woman return to her senses before Cassidy's baby was born?

Cassidy prayed that was the case.

"Eat more of that sandwich." Jenn raised her gun, her eyes hardening. "Don't make me tell you again."

Cassidy swallowed hard. "You can't shoot me. You need me alive."

Jenn scowled as if she knew Cassidy's words were true. But she still didn't lower the gun.

"Just eat! Don't make me angry. I might do something you won't like. That *I* won't like." Her words came out faster and faster. The woman was manic, wasn't she?

Cassidy took another bite and tried to chew.

But her abdominal muscles seized.

She nearly doubled over as they tightened.

Cassidy glanced up, realizing too late that she hadn't been able to cover her pain.

Jenn watched her, something igniting in her gaze. Excitement, maybe?

"What is it?" Jenn crept closer, her voice nearly breathless. "Is the baby coming?"

Cassidy sucked in a deep breath and tried her best to compose herself. "No. I think it's whatever you gave me. It's causing me to feel ill. What if I need a doctor?"

"You don't need a doctor! Women have been giving birth for centuries without doctors. I'll be here to help you. I can catch the baby when it comes out." The woman sounded as if she'd convinced herself the words were true.

Sweat spread across Cassidy's brow as the spasm continued—and at the thought of this woman helping deliver her baby.

Finally, the contraction subsided.

Cassidy drew in another deep breath.

How much longer would she be able to cover up the fact she could be going into labor? Jenn was watching her like a hawk. Certainly, she'd realize the truth sometime soon.

That meant Cassidy needed desperately to figure out what her plan was going to be.

15

GRIFF MCINTYRE

AS GRIFF MCINTYRE went door-to-door with his colleague Dez Rodriquez, he couldn't stop thinking about his own baby. Henry was born two weeks ago, and the child was so precious and vulnerable.

Then he thought about his wife, Bethany, and their daughter, Ada. Those three people were his whole world. If anything happened to them, he couldn't imagine how he would go on.

As his jaw tightened, he pulled his jacket higher around his neck to fight off the wind. It was unusually cold out here tonight, and he prayed Cassidy was somewhere safe and warm, not out in these elements.

He'd asked Bethany to stay inside with the kids and the doors locked while he searched the island for answers. But he knew Bethany was worried about Cassidy.

Cassidy meant a lot to her friends. She touched nearly everyone she met, and there wasn't a person Griff knew who wouldn't do everything possible to find her now.

Braden had thought they had a lead on who might have done this—a woman who'd come into The Crazy Chefette. But after talking to the waitress who'd served her, they discovered the woman had paid cash.

That meant they still didn't have a name yet.

He sighed.

Griff paused at the corner of the main highway and one of the smaller lanes leading toward the ocean.

He and Dez had already covered five streets in their designated search area. Most of the houses were empty. He couldn't remember the exact occupancy rate during the off-season, but most of these houses were rentals.

"The lights are on at that place." Dez nodded toward a house at the end of Seagull Lane.

"It's worth checking out."

Someone somewhere had to have seen *something*. They just needed to find that person.

Griff rang the doorbell at the house, and several minutes later a man and woman in their sixties answered.

The woman pulled on her pink house robe as she stared at them cautiously. "Can I help you?"

"We're sorry to disturb you so late," Griff started.

"I'm Griff, and this is Dez. Unfortunately, we have a missing woman on the island, and we're one of several search teams looking for her."

"I'm Linda, and this is my husband, Joe. That's terrible. What can we do to help?"

He held up his phone, which held a picture of Cassidy. "Have you seen this woman?"

Linda's eyes widened. "Isn't that . . . the police chief?"

"That's right. Cassidy Chambers." Griff used her name to make Cassidy seem more like a real person instead of a stranger. "Do you know her?"

"I wouldn't say I know her, but she helped me when my car was broken into a couple months ago. Seems like a nice woman. Pregnant too, right?" Linda's lips pulled down in a frown.

Griff's stomach tightened at the reminder. "That's correct."

Linda's frown deepened as she shook her head. "I've been inside all day. My husband and I are painting the house before the family arrives on Christmas. Unfortunately, we got behind schedule, and now we're scrambling to finish. Anyway, I wish I could tell you something that would help. I really do."

Disappointment bit into Griff, but he tried not to show it. "I appreciate your time. Just out of curiosity, have you seen anything suspicious happening around here?"

She paused a moment, and her gaze wavered back and forth as if in thought.

"I thought I saw someone at that house over there." Linda pointed to an oceanfront house one lane over. "I could be mistaken, but when I glanced outside to watch the sunset earlier, it looked like someone was walking beneath it."

Griff's breath caught. "Is that right?"

She frowned almost apologetically. "It could be just someone thinking rental property is fair game to explore. I've seen that happen before. People just assume they can look around if the place isn't being rented. It's probably nothing."

"Or it could be something." Griff stared at the dark, three-story structure in the distance. The lead was worth checking out. "Thank you so much for your help."

"Of course . . ."

Griff needed to call Officer Dillinger and see about getting a warrant to get inside that house.

Now.

16

CASSIDY CHAMBERS

CASSIDY FROZE as she heard a noise in the distance.

Jenn's body tensed as she seemed to hear it also.

"Cassidy?" someone shouted.

Dillinger.

That was Dillinger!

Cassidy started to scream.

But, before she could, Jenn shoved the door closed and threw her body against it.

She turned to Cassidy, something off-balance glittering in her eyes. "They'll never hear you."

Cassidy knew this was a soundproof room. But did that mean it was *absolutely* soundproof? She didn't know.

But she wasn't going to take this woman's word for it.

She dragged herself to her feet and began banging on the walls. "Help! I'm in here! Please!"

Jenn remained leaning against the door and watched Cassidy, almost as if she were entertained. She didn't try to stop her.

Her unwavering cockiness sent a chill up Cassidy's spine.

But she wasn't going to let that deter her.

Cassidy continued pounding on the walls and shouting.

Then she waited for someone to rush to the room.

But she heard nothing.

Nothing?

How was that even possible? Was this room truly that soundproof?

Tears pressed at her eyes as the truth tried to take center stage in her mind.

"That's enough. I really don't want you to upset the baby." Jenn's voice cut through the silence. "Getting all worked up like this isn't wise. I think you know that, don't you, Cassidy?"

Cassidy glanced at Jenn, rage rushing through her veins. Getting worked up wasn't good for the baby? How about being abducted? Held captive?

She kept that quiet, not wanting to waste time with an argument that wouldn't lead anywhere.

Instead, she began pounding the walls again.

This could be her only chance.

She couldn't let the opportunity slip away.

"Can anyone hear me? Please! I'm in here."

Still, nothing happened.

Jenn's expression grew irritated. The next moment, she pulled out her phone and stared at the screen. "You can stop now. They're gone."

"Gone?" Certainly Cassidy hadn't heard correctly. How did Jenn know that?

The pounding. The shouting.

Had Dillinger heard any of it?

Jenn showed her the phone screen, which displayed security footage from outside the house.

Dillinger, Griff, and Dez walked down the stairs, leaving the house and moving on.

A cry escaped Cassidy's lips.

They'd been close. *So* close.

Yet they hadn't heard her.

All the hope Cassidy had felt seemed to disappear.

If they hadn't been able to find her when they'd been mere feet away, what made Cassidy think someone would find her at all?

She could cry out with labor pains, and the only one who would hear her was God . . . and Jenn.

17

JACK WILSON

AS PASTOR JACK WILSON and his wife walked down the dark street cutting through the center of town, he continued to pray.

Dear Lord, watch over Cassidy. Protect her. Help the people searching for her here on the island to find her safe and unharmed.

He gripped Juliette's hand as he led a search party.

A group of thirteen others from church had joined them to help look for Cassidy. None of them were trained officers of the law, so they'd been instructed to be hands-off. Instead of going house to house, they'd walk the streets looking for anything out of place.

They were helping—just doing so in prayer.

They'd been planning on doing a prayer walk through the island anyway. It was a tradition the church had started a couple of years ago. Members would carry candles, sing carols, and pray blessings over each home they passed.

Tonight, the island felt quiet.

A chilly wind had nixed their candles. The salty air wasn't a normal Christmas scent, but it was comforting, nonetheless. Many houses had Christmas lights strung across their rooflines or on the small trees out front. Several had blow-up figures that danced in the breeze.

"It was only three years ago when we met and married." Juliette's soft voice was like a balm to his heart as she cut into his thoughts.

He smiled. Their attraction had been instant, and they'd married quickly—some would say too quickly. But Jack didn't regret it—not then and not now. Marrying Juliette had been one of the best decisions of his life.

"It seems like just yesterday in some ways, doesn't it?" he murmured.

She squeezed his hand tighter. "It does. At times, that situation we were in seemed hopeless. Yet God prevailed. God is going to prevail tonight for Cassidy also."

"Yes, He will." His wife's reassurance only confirmed what he already felt. God was in control, and Jack was believing for a miracle.

As they continued to walk down the quiet street stretching through the center of town, Juliette glanced at her watch. "It's almost Christmas Eve. Everybody should be home right now and getting ready for all their family celebrations."

"But the fact that so many people are out right now helping is a true testament to Cassidy. We're all pulling together to make sure she's okay."

"I'm so worried for her, Jack." Juliette frowned.

"I am too." Jack kept his voice low so members of his congregation wouldn't hear. "The situation doesn't sound good. But Christmas is the time for miracles. It started with the miracle of God being born in human flesh. His miracles have continued throughout the years. We can't stop believing and hoping now."

Juliette squeezed his hand harder. "You're right. We can't."

As they continued to walk, one of the congregants softly began singing "Silent Night."

As they reached the line about all being calm and bright, Jack was reminded of the importance of putting his trust in God—just as Mary and Joseph had done all those years ago.

18

AUTUMN SPENSER

AUTUMN SPENSER LOOKED up from the front desk at the Lantern Beach Medical Clinic as she typed her notes into the computer.

Mac MacArthur strode toward her, his stormy expression in contrast to the cheery decorations around them. One of the nurses had decorated the clinic with garlands and pine-scented wreaths. "Joy to the World" played overhead, and local elementary school students had drawn their best Christmas art, which was now displayed on the walls.

But all her attention was on Mac right now.

"Mac," she murmured, turning away from the computer. "Are you okay?"

"*I'm* fine, but I can't say that for everyone." A grim expression stained his gaze. "I was looking for Doc

Clemson, but I didn't see him. He hasn't answered his phone."

"He had to do a house call. Jane Lemon had knee replacement surgery and is having a hard time walking, so he went to check on her. He should be back anytime now. Is there anything I can do?"

Mac let out a sigh of resignation. "You heard about Cassidy?"

Autumn's lips pulled down in a frown at the mention of her friend's name. "I did. I wish I could do something. But I can't leave the clinic tonight."

"I understand."

She leaned closer, trying to keep her voice low in case anyone was listening. "When Cassidy is found, Doc Clemson and I will be there for her—whatever she needs. We're on call and at the ready, as military folks would say."

"I know you will be there. But I had another question for you." Mac shifted as if hesitant.

"Go ahead." She waited, sensing bad news was coming.

Mac frowned again before rubbing his hand over his forehead. "We believe Cassidy was knocked out and drugged, and I'm curious to know what that will do to a pregnant woman."

"Drugged?" Autumn tried to keep the shock out of her voice.

Mac nodded somberly, grief saturating his gaze.

She leaned against the desk in front of her, feeling weary at the thought of what Cassidy might be going through. Weary and horrified.

How could someone do this to her?

"Without knowing what the drug was, I can't say I know for sure what the effects would be," Autumn finally said. "But, in my professional opinion, any kind of stress like this could bring on early labor." She swallowed hard. "Or worse."

The lines on Mac's face grew deeper. "That's what I'm afraid of."

"We've got to find her, Mac."

His jaw tightened as he nodded. "We're doing everything in our power. Believe me, we are."

The problem was time wasn't on their side right now.

Especially not if Cassidy had been thrown into early labor.

19

TY CHAMBERS

TY HAD DRIVEN two hours south, just as he told himself he would. But those two hours had felt like the longest of his entire life. All he wanted was to get back home and look for his wife and his baby.

His heart pulsed rapidly. His blood pressure felt high. His nerves were raw.

He hadn't felt like this in a long time, not since his days fighting as a SEAL in the Middle East.

He pulled into a small airport located in Louisville and climbed out. A sharp wind still hit him, but at least it wasn't snowing here like in Indianapolis. He hoped he might be able to find a flight. He'd pay whatever someone was asking if it meant getting home to Cassidy sooner.

When he went inside and finally reached the ticketing agent, he learned that the earliest flight available didn't leave until in the morning.

He fisted his hands as frustration built inside him. There had to be *something* he could do.

Ty paused near a waiting area as he tried to collect his thoughts.

"You looking to get back quicker?"

Ty turned and saw a man probably in his fifties, with a salt-and-pepper beard and thinning hair, standing behind him.

He had no idea who this guy was, but it couldn't hurt to talk for a few minutes.

"I am," he said. "Ty Chambers."

"I'm Larry Baskins. I do private charters. I was going to head home for the evening, but you sound desperate. I couldn't help but overhear what you were saying to the agent at the desk."

Ty would explore every opportunity right now—even if it seemed shady. "I need to go to Lantern Beach, North Carolina."

"The island?" Larry twisted his lips as if that would be a challenge. "Not an easy place to land. In fact, I don't think there are any air strips there."

"I know of a place—but it would take a little talent." The Blackout headquarters was in the process of developing a small landing strip. It wasn't quite done, but it could still work.

The man raised his eyebrows. "Is that right? That's got to be at least a five-hour flight."

"I know. But my wife is pregnant and in trouble. I need to get back to her."

Larry seemed to still at his words. "What kind of trouble?"

"We believe somebody abducted her."

Larry's eyes widened. "I'm sorry to hear that. I lost my wife fifteen years ago. That's something that a person doesn't forget."

"So, you understand what I'm facing right now." Was this guy considering flying him home?

The man slowly nodded before glancing out the window at the airstrip on the other side. "The weather isn't ideal, but I think my plane can handle it—if you're willing to take that risk. But if it gets too choppy out there, I'm going to have to come down."

Ty's heart thrummed with anticipation. "I understand. But I'm willing to try if you are."

"It's going to take me a few minutes to get things lined up, so just hold tight."

Ty lifted a prayer of thanks for God's provision. Then he began praying he'd get back in time to help . .

.

But mostly he prayed for Cassidy and their baby.

20

ELISE LOCKE

AS ELISE LOCKE sat in a rocking chair in the dark nursery, she picked up her phone to call her husband, Colton. She hated to interrupt him in the middle of his search and rescue efforts. But she had to know if there were any updates.

Her own baby, Ivy, was only a month old. She, Bethany, and Cassidy had all been thrilled to find out they'd be pregnant together. But now, that fact was a grim reminder that life sometimes had different plans.

No, Elise, don't think like that.

As a psychologist, Elise knew the power of thoughts. She needed to stay positive right now. Cassidy was going to be okay, no matter how grim this situation seemed.

Colton answered on the first ring. "Hey, honey. Is everything okay?"

Of course, his first thought was to worry something was wrong. She couldn't blame him after everything that had happened.

"We're fine." Elise gazed at the precious baby girl sleeping in her arms. Normally, she would put Ivy in the crib. But, tonight, she just needed to hold her daughter a little longer. "I just needed to know if there were any updates. I'm sorry to disturb you."

"You never disturb me. And, no, there aren't any updates. We thought we might have found the location where Cassidy was taken, but no one was inside. We're still looking."

Elise frowned, fighting the despair that wanted to kick in. "I'm sorry to hear that. I was really hoping for a timely resolution to this."

"We all are. But we're still out here searching and trying to figure out what's going on."

She gazed down at Ivy's peaceful face as the baby's lips made a suckling sound. "Do you think this is about Cassidy's baby?"

"It's our best guess right now." Colton's words sounded grim, as if they tattered his spirit as he said them aloud.

At once, a thought hit Elise and she stiffened. "Colton . . ."

"What is it?"

"Yesterday, I was at Peyton's bakery with Ivy when a woman approached me. She told me she wanted to pick up some babysitting jobs and said if I needed someone, I should call her."

"What did you tell her?"

"I thought she seemed harmless, so I just smiled and nodded—not that I had any intention of using her." Elise's heart sped at the thought.

"What did she do?"

Elise clearly remembered the meeting. The woman had seemed overly eager and almost awkward as she'd stood too close for comfort. "She asked if she could hold Ivy. But I didn't let her, of course."

"I don't like how that sounds."

"It was strange. She didn't push, but she did give me her phone number."

"What?" Colton rushed. "Do you still have it?"

"It should be in my purse."

"I'm going to need that number, Elise." Colton's voice lifted with hope.

"Of course. I'll put Ivy down and find it." She wedged the phone between her shoulder and ear and stood.

"Tell me—what did this woman look like?"

Elise briefly closed her eyes as she pictured the woman. "She was probably five foot eight. On the sturdy side, if that makes sense. She had short, dark hair and a deep voice." She paused. "Do you think this might help you find Cassidy?"

"If we can track down the name of the woman it

will help. Maybe we can even trace her cell phone and ping the signal to her current location."

Elise gently placed Ivy in the crib, thankful her daughter was a heavy sleeper. "I'll go find it now and text it to you."

"Thanks, honey. I love you." Colton's voice deepened until he almost sounded hoarse. "Give my baby girl a kiss good night for me."

She gazed down at Ivy again, and warmth filled her heart. "I will. Find Cassidy for us, Colton. Please."

21

JIMMY JAMES GAMBLE

CAPTAIN JIMMY JAMES GAMBLE walked to his front door as he heard someone pounding on it.

Who would be here at this time of night? It had to be close to midnight. Thankfully, he hadn't gone to bed yet. He'd been too busy trying to wrap Christmas gifts. They all looked horrible. The edges were uneven, the paper wrinkled, and the tape ran in all directions.

He'd be better off sticking with tying knots at the marina than trying to make his presents look pretty. Even the shiny big bows on top didn't help.

He bristled as he opened the door. He'd halfway expected to see trouble standing there.

Instead, Axel Hendrix stared at him.

Axel worked for Blackout, but the two of them had hit it off while talking about motorcycles. The man had a bit of a rebel vibe, which was probably why Jimmy

James got along with him so well. Jimmy James liked to refer to himself as "reformed," mostly because Kenzie Anderson had come into his life.

She'd made him a better man.

In fact, this year—for the first time in probably a decade—Jimmy James had actually decorated his house for Christmas. With Kenzie's help, of course.

"Axel." Jimmy James let down his guard but only slightly. "You know what time it is, right?"

Axel didn't crack a smile. "Cassidy's missing."

Alarm raced through Jimmy James. "What? Come inside and tell me what's going on."

Axel stepped inside but remained near the door, his posture tense and his voice urgent as he explained what had happened.

With the new details, Jimmy James' gut tightened.

"What can I do?" Jimmy James crossed his arms over his chest. He'd always liked Cassidy. She had believed in him and given him a chance when no one else would.

"We're trying to track down any information that might help us. Has anything suspicious happened at the marina lately?"

"Anything suspicious?" Jimmy James' thoughts raced. "As you know, *Diamond of the Seas* is docked here for the next few months. It's too cold to do any charters, so I've mostly been taking it easy. Kenzie and I have been restoring some old boats to sell."

"I figured you weren't running any charters right now, but I wanted to ask, just in case."

A memory hit Jimmy James. "Now that you mention it, a woman *did* stop by the marina office yesterday to talk to me a few minutes. I'm not sure if it had anything to do with this or not."

Curiosity lit Axel's gaze. "Tell me, just in case."

"She didn't give me her name. But she was pregnant and kept rubbing her belly. If I had to guess, she was in her mid to late twenties. She was heavyset with dark hair. She asked if I might be able to let her charter *Diamond of the Seas* to take up north on Christmas."

"On Christmas day?" Axel narrowed his eyes. "Why was she asking something like that at the last minute? And while she's pregnant?"

"I had all the same questions, but I didn't feel like it was my place to ask." Jimmy James shrugged.

"Was she alone?"

"That was the other thing. She *was* by herself, which I thought was strange. Most pregnant women don't travel alone on a yacht."

"What did you tell her?"

"I explained I wasn't working on Christmas day and that my girlfriend's family was in town, so we'd be spending the holiday together."

Axel's eyes narrowed with thought. "How did she react?"

Jimmy James recalled the conversation well. "She

looked irritated, which I thought was an overreaction especially since she'd come to me last minute. Then she told me what she would pay me if I could do it."

"How much?"

"A hundred thousand."

Axel's eyebrows shot up. "That's a pretty penny if I've ever seen one."

"Luxury comes at a price. But I still told her I couldn't do it. She gave me a dirty look and stomped away." Jimmy James shrugged. "And that was that."

"Did she say where she was going?"

Jimmy James let out a long breath as he replayed their conversation. "I'm pretty sure she said her family has a place here on Lantern Beach."

Axel's eyes lit. "Is that right? That could be helpful. Because we've been searching the records of all the rentals. But if it's an owner . . . then this woman would stay at the house they own . . . which will make things a lot more difficult."

22

CASSIDY CHAMBERS

CASSIDY WAS RUNNING out of options.

She stared at the room around her as she sagged against the wall. Alone.

Jenn had left several minutes ago, giving Cassidy a moment to collect herself.

But she couldn't just sit here. She needed to do something.

She could yell all she wanted, but no one could hear her. The room she occupied was clearly concealed. If it wasn't, then Dillinger, Griff and Dez would have tried the door when they came earlier.

That meant if Cassidy was going to get out of this alive and with her baby, she'd have to take action herself.

Cassidy rubbed her belly again and lifted a prayer. Usually, she felt certain about her decisions and didn't second-guess herself. But right now, she couldn't seem to stop herself from doing that. The last thing she wanted was to put her baby in danger.

No ideal solutions had come to mind. But there had to be *something* she was missing.

Her impression was that Jenn didn't want to harm her baby. She simply wanted to take Cassidy's child and run away to start her own life.

Her gut told her she wouldn't survive after giving birth—not if Jenn had anything to do with it.

A cry welled in her chest at the thought.

The last thing Cassidy wanted was for her baby to grow up without a mother. She wouldn't let that happen.

The thing was . . . this woman was unstable. Cassidy's baby wouldn't be safe with Jenn. She had no doubt about that.

She wrestled with knowing the best thing to do—with knowing how to protect both herself and her child. But she knew one thing for certain. As soon as Cassidy saw the opportunity to act, she couldn't miss it.

Earlier, Jenn had insisted on watching Cassidy eat the sandwich and drink the water, overly concerned about Cassidy's health.

Cassidy had finished her dinner as directed. But now she felt sick to her stomach. She didn't think it was because Jenn had put anything in her drink or food. The entire situation was making her queasy.

And the pregnancy.

As another contraction tightened her abdomen, Cassidy pressed her eyes closed. Sweat spread across her forehead, and she tried to control her breathing, just like Doc Clemson had taught her.

The two of them, unfortunately, hadn't gone over any possible scenario where Cassidy might go into labor in a soundproof room with only a psychopath to help her.

Cassidy might laugh—only there was nothing funny about this.

She leaned her head back against the wall and counted to twenty.

Finally, the contraction passed.

But she was having them more regularly. Probably every ten or fifteen minutes if she had to guess.

Her heart rate quickened at the thought.

She couldn't have her baby in here. Not with Jenn. Not without Ty.

She squeezed her eyes shut. *Dear Lord, please give me wisdom. Protect my baby. I'm begging You.*

Opening her eyes again, she swallowed hard. Jenn's image flashed through her mind. The woman was probably thirty pounds heavier than Cassidy and athletic. She also had a gun.

Jenn definitely had the upper hand in the situation since Cassidy didn't even know exactly where she was. Based on the video Jenn had shown her of Dillinger and the guys leaving, Cassidy guessed she was in one of the beach houses stretching down the sandy shores of the island.

That was good news, at least. If she escaped, she would know where to find help.

But, first, her priority had to be getting out of here. She would figure out the rest from there. With nothing to use as a weapon, that meant she had only her own body to use—with her baby inside.

She sighed.

She couldn't risk her child.

It felt like a no-win situation.

The minutes ticked past. Or maybe it was seconds.

Time seemed simultaneously slow and fast.

Another contraction came and went.

Cassidy glanced at the camera in the corner. Was Jenn watching her right now?

The last thing Cassidy wanted was for that woman to know she could be going into labor.

She fought with everything inside her to keep her expression neutral. To control her breathing. To not give any hints as to what was happening.

Just then, the door opened again, and Jenn stood in the opening with a wide, hopeful grin on her face. "How's my baby doing?"

Disgust churned inside Cassidy.

The life growing inside her was *not* Jenn's. It never would be.

"I need to use the bathroom." Cassidy squeezed her expression to drive home her dilemma.

Jenn shrugged apathetically. "I know this isn't sanitary, but you're going to have to do it in the corner. Soon, nothing that happens in this room will matter. Only your baby."

Cassidy swallowed the bitterness rising in her. "I can't use the bathroom in here. There's not even a bucket. Besides, if the baby is born here, he or she can't be born into filth. Everything needs to be sterile."

"Finally, you said *he or she*. Why did you keep calling the baby *it* earlier? Don't you love the child enough to refer to the baby as a person?"

Cassidy rubbed her stomach. The anxiety she felt couldn't be good for her baby. "I love my child very much. But I don't know yet if I'm having a boy or a girl. Ty and I want to be surprised."

Jenn made a pouty face. "That's *so sweet*. But it's not going to matter anymore, is it?"

Cassidy's heart sped again. She needed a plan—and she needed it now.

"I need to use the bathroom," she repeated. "It's an emergency. The baby is pressing on my bladder."

Jenn remained silent a moment as if contemplating her options. Finally, she muttered, "How do I know you're not going to try anything?"

"I'm pregnant. What am I going to try to do?" Cassidy rubbed her belly again, playing on her vulnerable state and hoping to use it to her advantage. It helped that she really did have to use the restroom.

Jenn narrowed her eyes. "I don't know. You're smart. You could try something."

"I just need to go to the bathroom." Desperation tinged Cassidy's voice. "Please."

Jenn continued to study her a moment before nodding. "Fine. Get up. But don't try anything."

23

DANE BRADSHAW

OFFICER DANE BRADSHAW sat at his desk, acting as the point person for any new information that came in.

People had been calling in tips, and search parties had been directed to contact him with updates. His job was to sort through all the information and make sure nothing was overlooked.

But the last call he'd received had caught his interest.

Colton had told him about the woman who'd approached Elise and given her phone number for potential babysitting.

It seemed like their best lead yet.

Dane plugged the number into the system and held his breath.

They just needed a break. Just one. Then maybe they could find Cassidy and her soon-to-be-born baby.

He expelled a breath as results populated his computer screen.

That phone number wasn't a burner phone.

It was registered to someone.

A woman named Jenn Brentwood. Twenty-eight-years old. From Connecticut.

Dane scanned the rest of her information, trying to sort out what might be helpful.

Jenn was from a wealthy family who owned a textile business. She'd never been married and had trouble holding down a job. She had some experience in the tech field. However, it appeared she lived off her family's wealth.

A picture of the woman popped onto Dane's screen.

His breath caught.

This was it.

She matched the description he'd been given of Cassidy's abductor.

Now they had confirmation of a name to go with the face.

Dane just needed to call in some contacts and see if they could get a trace on the number. Maybe they could pinpoint this woman's location.

Then he needed to call the rest of the gang with an update about what was going on.

24

WES O'NEILL

WES SAT BESIDE HIS FIANCÉE, Paige Henderson. She was the dispatcher at the police station, and she was manning the phone lines right now.

He wanted to support her, so he'd brought some coffee and a banana nut muffin. This was looking like it would be a long night.

Cassidy had been missing for almost five hours now.

Cassidy and Ty were part of the weekly Bible study Wes attended. The members had grown close and felt like family. In fact, Cassidy was practically like a sister to him.

The phone rang again, and Paige answered. "Lantern Beach Police Department."

Wes listened as Paige jotted notes.

Something changed in her gaze.

After Paige transferred the call to Dillinger, she turned back toward Wes. "A woman who's here visiting her grandmother said she saw some suspicious activity at a house earlier today. She said, by the looks of the place, no one is staying there, but she saw someone go inside."

Wes' pulse quickened. "Is there a car parked outside it now?"

"She said there's not," Paige said. "But it's the same house Dillinger got a search warrant to check earlier. He said it was clear, that no one was there, and that there was no evidence that anyone had been there."

"Two hits on the same house is probably significant."

"That's what I thought too. I hope they find Cassidy there."

Wes prayed the same thing . . . because they desperately needed some answers.

25

CASSIDY CHAMBERS

AS SOON AS Jenn stepped into the soundproof room, Cassidy saw her opportunity.

She rammed Jenn into the wall.

The woman stumbled to the floor. As she did, Cassidy dashed toward the door. If she could just get outside, maybe she could yell for help.

This was the only thing she could think of. Her only chance to get out of here.

Just as her hand connected with the doorknob, Jenn shouted, "Stop right there!"

Cassidy threw the door open anyway.

As she did, she heard a gun cock.

Jenn was going to shoot her.

Before she could, the gun came down on Cassidy's head and she fell to the floor.

A cry of despair wanted to escape. Instead, it lodged in her throat.

Jenn leaned over her, shaking her head with a sneer. "Look what you made me do. That can't be good for the baby."

Cassidy wanted to open her mouth. Wanted to cry for help. To do something to get attention.

But she couldn't move or speak. Not right now.

Jenn grabbed her arms and began dragging her limp body back into the soundproof room then left Cassidy sprawled on the floor.

Just as Cassidy's head cleared, she felt a *whoosh*.

Her breath caught.

The pool beneath her confirmed her water had broken.

This baby was coming . . . soon.

26

GABE MICHAELS

GABE STOOD in the police station as an impromptu meeting occurred. All the search parties were back, but no one had found anything. Every street had been searched. People had been questioned.

But there was nothing.

Their only lead was the call to the station a half hour ago about suspicious activity at an otherwise empty house.

"I searched inside that house with Griff and Dez," Braden said as he stood at the front of the group, taking charge of the situation. "We didn't find anyone there."

Griff shook his head. "We looked in the closets, behind doors, *everywhere.*"

"Not only did someone else see some movement

there earlier today, but Jenn Brentwood's cell phone is also pinging from that location," Dane stated.

"I just don't know where Cassidy could have been," Dez said. "We yelled. Cassidy would have alerted us if she were inside."

"I know—unless she was unable to." Braden pressed his lips together until they formed a grim line. "But this is all we've got right now."

Gabe's mind continued to race as he thought about the situation. "What's the update on Ty?"

"He chartered a plane and is on his way back," Colton said. "Let's just hope the weather holds out. A plane that small is difficult to fly in any type of wind. The last thing we need is two tragedies on our hands."

The thought of something also happening to Ty made Gabe's head pound.

Griff turned toward him. "What about that thermal imaging technology on that new drone you got?"

Gabe shrugged. "What about it?"

"What if you flew the drone over the house? Could you see if someone was inside?"

He thought about it for a moment before nodding. "I should be able to. But with these winds, it's going to be hard to operate."

"If anyone can do it, it's you."

Gabe appreciated his vote of confidence, but the elements weren't on his side right now. "I'm willing to see what I can do. I'll drive back to the Blackout campus and get it. Then I'll meet you at the house."

"That sounds good." Colton's gaze locked with his. "We don't have any time to waste."

Gabe nodded and rushed outside to his car.

He knew this was a longshot.

But maybe it would work.

He prayed it would.

27

ERNESTINE SANDERS

ERNESTINE FELT relief flush through her when she saw Doc Clemson standing in her doorway. Not only was she dating Clemson, but she'd been worried when she'd heard about the excitement on the island.

"I finished my house calls and stopped by the clinic for a while," he explained as he took off his coat. "I'm sorry it's so late."

"I'm just glad you're here."

As the former editor of the local newspaper, *The Lantern Beach Outlook,* Ernestine, who still acted as publisher, had already gotten several calls. Cassidy's abduction had been all the talk around the island.

Her nephew, Webster Newsome, who was the current editor, and his girlfriend, Serena Lavinia, had come to her house so they could begin drafting an article.

These were the kinds of stories Ernestine didn't like to write. Seeing people she cared about in danger was hard to stomach.

Ernestine ushered Clemson to the kitchen table and poured him some peppermint tea to ward away the chill in the air. Webster and Serena also sat at the table, Serena holding her dog, Scoops, in her lap.

After Clemson had taken several sips, Ernestine dove into her questions. "Are there any updates you can share?"

Doc Clemson gave her a brief overview of what he knew.

Ernestine took a sip of her tea. "So, the police think Cassidy might be in this house, but they've checked it and didn't find her?"

Clemson frowned and scrubbed a hand over his face. "That's right. They're trying to use thermal imaging to see if anyone's inside. But if Cassidy's not there, I don't think they know where else to look."

"What house?" Serena rushed, her eyebrows knitted together.

As the resident newspaper reporter and ice cream woman, Serena knew the island well.

"The one over on Ocean Shoals," Clemson said. "The big one on the ocean."

Ernestine could picture the place perfectly. "I'm familiar with that one. I believe they call it the Squawking Gull."

"How do you know that?" Clemson narrowed his eyes with curiosity.

"I've lived here a long time. Done lots of stories on homeowners and famous guests and everything in between."

"What else do you know about it?"

Ernestine tapped a pen against her lips as she thought. "It's a very memorable house. The man who built it twenty-five years ago was a music producer."

Clemson seemed to freeze with curiosity. "Tell me more."

"He was part of some label, and he'd bring his artists here to record. But I think he had some financial problems and ended up selling the place about fifteen years ago. I'm not exactly sure who bought it. But I don't think it was anyone affiliated with the music world. Who knows what happened to that old studio?"

Serena's voice caught with excitement. "The house might still have a soundproof room."

"But wouldn't law enforcement have seen that space when they were in the house?" Webster pushed his glasses up higher on his nose.

"You would think," Serena said. "But what if someone did an easy fix? What if the new owner bought the place, knew that vacationers wouldn't care about a music studio, and, instead of doing a major renovation, they simply covered the room up somehow?"

Ernestine's heart rate quickened. "I think you might be onto something."

"I think so too." Doc glanced at his watch. "Now that you say that, I'm going to head to the house just in case they find Cassidy. I want to be close when they do. She might need me after everything she's been through."

Ernestine reached up and patted him affectionately on the cheek. "You do that. But promise me you'll take good care of yourself in the process."

"Yes, ma'am."

As he left, Ernestine clutched her hands in front of her. At this moment, all thoughts about publishing her next article disappeared. All she cared about was Cassidy and her baby.

28

TY CHAMBERS

TY GLANCED out the window of the small puddle jumper at the dark sky outside. This had been the longest—and hardest—flight of his life.

"I'm about to start our descent," Larry said into his headset.

Ty had been on shaky flights before. But this was one of the worst. More than once, Larry had almost done an emergency landing. Then the wind would clear a moment and they kept going.

But Ty knew this landing would be tricky. He'd already let the guys at Blackout know to be ready for them.

Not only were weather conditions less than ideal, but the runway would require expert skill. It wasn't quite ready yet. But it would have to work.

Ty would like to think that Larry was cut out for the job, but he couldn't say that with certainty. He didn't know the man well enough to know that.

As another gust of wind sent the plane on an airborne roller coaster, Ty gripped his armrest and tried to steady his breathing.

This would all be worth it if he could get to Cassidy in time. That had been his prayer for the entire trip.

"Here we go." Larry gripped the yoke then hit several switches.

Ty knew the turbulence would get worse as they dipped lower in the atmosphere. And he was right. The wind pushed the plane back and forth, up and down.

He continued praying.

In the distance, he saw a smattering of small lights on the ground.

Lantern Beach.

That had to be Lantern Beach.

Ty hadn't been able to get any updates while in the air, and that fact was killing him. He wanted to know what was going on and if there were any new developments.

He was trying to be patient. To be patient and trust God with all this.

But this just might be his biggest test of faith ever.

Larry muttered a few things into his radio.

Then the pilot glanced at him. "Are you a praying man?"

"I am."

"Then you better start right now and ask God for His help in making this landing. Because I'm not sure I can do it on my own."

29

CASSIDY CHAMBERS

PAIN LIKE CASSIDY had never felt before ripped through her abdomen.

She'd been trying to count the time between her contractions.

Four minutes apart. That was her best guess.

What did that mean? How much time did she have until the baby came?

She couldn't remember anything right now.

Agony consumed her.

Jenn knelt in front of her with a wide grin on her face. She'd pulled on some gloves and had grabbed a baby blanket, a sheet, and scissors.

That was all she had for the birth of this baby.

Another cry lodged in her throat.

Cassidy tried not to let fear get the best of her.

But it was hard.

She didn't know how this situation was going to end, so all she could do was pray.

Lord, Your Son was born as a baby into this world in circumstances that seemed uncertain. Yet His birth transformed mankind as we know it. You kept Your promises to Mary and Joseph. Lord, I beg You now to watch over this baby of mine also. I haven't done anything to deserve any special favors. But I pray for Your grace and mercy on us now. Please.

As the prayer ended, a cry escaped from Cassidy—one that came from the depths of her soul. The sound was half shrouded in pain and half in fear. The pain . . . it felt unbearable.

"You can do this," Jenn tried to coach her. "Just push."

Cassidy wasn't sure if she was ready to push. What if something was wrong? What if it was too early? Or if the cord was wrapped around her baby's neck?

"I need a doctor," she muttered.

"You don't need a doctor," Jenn growled. "Like I said, you have me."

"But you don't know what you're doing." As soon as Cassidy said the words, she regretted them. The last thing she needed was to set this woman off.

"Don't insult me right now! I'm the only person here to help you. You don't want to put yourself on my bad side, do you?"

Cassidy swallowed hard and tried to control her breathing.

The baby was going to come, and there was nothing that she could do to stop it.

30

BECKETT JONES

"WHAT DO YOU HAVE SO FAR?" Beckett leaned closer to Gabe as his colleague sent a drone into the windy atmosphere.

The whole team—including police officers and Blackout members—had set up at a house on the other side of the sand dune. It was out of sight from anyone inside the house on Ocean Shoals. But they were close enough to act when it came time.

The two of them stared at the screen Gabe held in both hands.

"You're going to have to be patient with me," Gabe muttered. "The wind keeps pushing the drone around. I'll be lucky if I don't lose this thing to the ocean."

"Keep trying," Beckett said. "You can do it."

But Gabe had made it clear he wasn't all that sure about how successful he would be.

A moment later, Autumn Spenser appeared beside him. She reached up and kissed his cheek.

"You've got this," she muttered to him. "I have no doubt about that."

His whole countenance brightened at her attention. She'd always had that effect on Junior.

"Thanks for your vote of confidence." Gabe cast a soft smile at her. "I didn't think you could be here."

"I'm on call, but I was able to slip away for a while." Autumn squeezed his arm. "I wanted to be here to help however I could."

Gabe stared at the screen he held.

Beckett knew enough to know that the monitor was the only thing Gabe had to let him know where exactly the drone was going. He let his colleague have some space so he could concentrate.

"Got it," Gabe finally muttered.

Beckett leaned closer. The drone was finally on top of the Ocean Shoals house.

"I don't know how long I can hold this drone in place." Gabe's voice tightened. "But I'm going to try to keep it there long enough to see if there are any thermal images coming from inside."

"Just concentrate on holding steady," Beckett said. "The rest of us will worry about everything else."

Dating Samantha had taught Beckett a few things about patience. Right now, Samantha was staying with Elise, her best friend. Samantha had a way of calming people down, and Beckett knew that was what she was doing right now back at Blackout headquarters.

"Brandon just talked to the pilot on the radio." Colton approached them. "He's about to land at the Blackout headquarters. But they're having some trouble because of the wind."

"Who's there helping?" Beckett asked.

"Just our newest Blackout hire, Brandon. He has some experience flying, but without a control tower . . ."

Gabe hit something on his screen and, a moment later, Beckett saw two blobs appear on the screen.

His breath caught. "Is that what I think it is?"

Gabe nodded. "Two people are inside the house. It looks like they're somewhere in the center of the space."

"That doesn't make sense," Griff muttered. "Unless there really is some type of secret room that's sealed from the rest of the house."

"It's a studio," Colton reminded them. "The walls must be soundproof. Really soundproof."

"Now that we know that they're in there, what are we waiting for?" Beckett turned to the rest of the team, anxious to get started.

"Hopefully, Ty will be here at any moment," Dillinger said. "But we can't wait. We have got to move. Now."

Colton nodded. "I agree. Now that we know for sure someone's in there, we need to find Cassidy."

"We don't want to show our hand too soon," Dillinger said. "So we'll go in quietly. We don't know what this woman is capable of. The last thing we want to do is to set her off."

Beckett sucked in a breath, praying they handled this situation correctly.

Because more than one life was on the line right now.

And one misstep could be devastating.

31

CASSIDY CHAMBERS

TEARS FLOWED from Cassidy's eyes. She couldn't stop praying for her child. Couldn't stop thinking about everything she'd already overcome in her nearly three decades of life.

God had led her through many valleys.

He could lead her through this too.

Another cry of pain escaped from her.

The contractions were only two minutes apart now. Jenn kept on saying something about how she was crowning.

All Cassidy knew was that all the controlled breathing in the world wasn't helping her right now.

"My baby is coming," Jenn muttered, a touch of elation in her voice. "I can't believe it."

A surge of adrenaline rushed through Cassidy. This

baby wasn't going anywhere with Jenn. But she was helpless right now.

Her only hope was that God—and the people of Lantern Beach—would help her.

"You can do this," Jenn said. "Just keep letting Mother Nature do her job, and you'll be just fine."

With another scream of pain, Cassidy knew she had little choice but to listen to her body.

32

TY CHAMBERS

THE PLANE TOUCHED down at an angle and bounced back into the air.

It hit the ground a second time and lifted again.

Ty braced himself for the final impact—and he prayed it was a good one.

He made the mistake of glancing at Larry's face again. As the man eased back on the yoke, allowing the nose to dip a little without forcing it, trepidation lined his gaze.

Larry was scared too.

The last thing they needed was to go into a nosedive.

Finally, the plane touched down and stayed on the ground.

But they were going too fast.

Making the situation more difficult was the fact

that not all the runway lights had been installed yet. Larry was having to feel his way through the situation, not knowing exactly where the runway would end.

Larry kept close contact with Brandon on his radio as he navigated the air strip.

Ty pressed his eyes closed as the plane careened down the runway.

He prayed they'd stop in time—before they hit the trees at the end of the space.

But he wasn't certain that would happen.

"Hold on," Larry warned as he engaged the brakes.

Ty's entire body suddenly lunged forward.

Finally, they stopped moving.

Ty opened his eyes, halfway expecting to realize they'd crashed and he was in a state of shock.

But when he glanced over at Larry, he saw a grin spread across his face as he threw his hands in the air. "We did it!"

Ty reached over and gave the man a quick hug and pat on the back. "Good job."

"Now you need to get out of here."

Ty took off his headset and seatbelt. By the time he opened the door, Mac had already appeared to help him deplane.

Ty hurried down the steps and into the awaiting car.

"We think we found Cassidy in a rental house," Mac quickly told him as they took off down the road.

"You think? Has anyone seen her yet? Is she okay?" Ty's heart pounded in his ears as he waited for Mac's answer.

"We don't have eyes on her yet. We're acting on thermal images from Gabe's drone. The team is going in now. The place is only five minutes away."

"Then try to make it in three."

CASSIDY CHAMBERS

"I CAN SEE his or her head. Keep pushing." Jenn's words came out harsh, almost like a command.

"I'm doing my best," Cassidy muttered under her breath as her hands gripped her swollen stomach.

But the agony of childbirth had rendered her almost helpless.

All she could do was continue to pray.

Lord, please be with us now.

"You need to push harder," Jenn said.

"I'm pushing as hard as I can," Cassidy muttered.

"My baby is coming. Don't do anything to mess this up. You're not trying hard enough!"

Anything to mess this up? Not trying hard enough?

This woman must have truly lost her mind.

"I can't rush this." Cassidy's words sounded wispy with pain.

"Stop talking back!" Jenn reached over and grabbed her gun.

Then she aimed it at Cassidy—as if that would accelerate the childbirth process.

34

TY CHAMBERS

TY JUMPED out of the car before it came to a complete stop. There was no time to waste.

He rushed toward the men gathered beneath the house. He found Dillinger and Colton first.

Colton's hand came down on his shoulder, his gaze pensive. "Ty . . . glad you've made it, man."

"You're just in time," Dillinger said. "We're about to go in."

"I'm going with you," Ty said. "Don't try to talk me out of it."

"Wouldn't dream of it," Dillinger said. "Let's go."

Following behind Dillinger, Ty stepped into the dark beach house.

Everything was quiet around them.

This was the place where Cassidy was being kept? Were they sure?

Ty didn't have time to question them now. Right now, he simply needed to act.

He gripped his gun, just in case.

They searched the entire house—including every closet and alcove.

No one was here.

Ty paused in the living room and frowned, fighting the sense of despair that wanted to claim him.

"Thermal imaging showed us that two people were somewhere in the middle of the structure," Colton muttered as he scanned the space.

Ty glanced around. What were they missing?

He paced the living room, his heart thrumming in his ears.

Pausing near the stairway, he studied the area above him. The ceiling over the stairway on the third floor was lower than he expected.

Was that a design feature?

Or something more?

"Dillinger. Colton. Mac. This way!" Ty motioned for them to follow.

He took the steps by twos as he hurried upstairs. Four bedrooms were located up here, but they'd already checked those.

Ty focused on the space above the stairway.

To most people who looked at it, the design simply appeared to be a dropped ceiling.

But what if the studio was located there?

He paused at the top of the stairs.

He didn't see any doors or other ways to enter the space.

Dillinger lingered close. "What are you thinking?"

Ty stepped toward a large, full-length mirror mounted to the wall.

This had to be it. It was the only place where a door might be concealed.

He tugged at the mirror, but it didn't budge. It almost seemed as if it were glued to the wall

Strange.

Ty pushed into it.

When he did, the mirror swung inward, and a doorway opened before him.

35

CASSIDY CHAMBERS

CASSIDY LET out a cry as another contraction hit her. They were less than a minute apart now. One blended into the next, and she had no relief from the pain. No time to breathe and regroup. There was no doubt that her baby was coming.

She stared at Jenn, who still aimed the gun at her as if that would make Cassidy give birth faster. This woman was out of her mind.

But nature was doing what nature did best.

Cassidy's baby would soon be born.

As another contraction seized her abdomen, Cassidy froze.

Was that movement near the door? Or was she seeing things?

Her eyes widened even though she tried not to give away too much of what she was seeing.

Could it be . . . ?

She swallowed hard.

It was. The door had moved.

Someone was coming in.

Did Jenn have an accomplice?

Or . . .

Cassidy's breath left her lungs in a whoosh as Ty's face appeared.

Ty.

He was here!

She cried out again, partly with pain and partly in relief.

Maybe her prayers were answered. Maybe there was still hope.

In the blink of an eye, Jenn twirled around.

She pointed the gun at him and sneered. "One more step, and I'll shoot. Don't test me."

36

TY CHAMBERS

AS SOON AS Ty saw the gun, he knew this wouldn't be as simple as he'd hoped.

But Cassidy was on the floor about to give birth.

There was no time to waste. Even though he had a team behind him, there was no space in this room for all of them. Right now, it was just him, Cassidy, and this woman with the gun.

His heart rate quickened.

This was the moment they'd been waiting for.

Their baby was coming.

"Step back," the woman with the gun snapped again. "Don't test me."

The woman had a deranged look in her eyes. She meant those words. She would do something drastic if she were pushed.

Ty raised his hands. "I don't want to hurt you."

"Yeah, well, I'll hurt you." Spittle flew from her mouth. "I mean it."

"I know you do." He kept his voice calm. "I just need to help Cassidy."

"She has me. She doesn't need your help."

Ty swallowed hard, knowing he didn't have any time to waste. "She's in labor. She needs all the help she can get right now. She needs to get somewhere clean and sanitary where the baby will be given medical attention."

"He or she doesn't need any medical attention." Defiance stained her gaze—and cluelessness.

Had this woman had some kind of psychotic break? That was his best guess.

"You can do this, Cassidy." Ty looked back at his wife.

Sweat covered her brow, and her breaths came out short and clipped as she clutched her stomach. She had nothing to comfort her. No pillow. No cushions to lie on. Only the carpeted floor. A single sheet was draped over her, giving her minimal privacy.

This was not how this was supposed to go down.

He wanted nothing more than to be beside her.

But not right now.

He looked back at the woman. "The baby's going to need to be seen by a doctor. The stress of this situation can cause issues. Too much can go wrong."

The woman's expression seemed to crack for a moment. "You don't know what you're talking about."

"Yes, I do. I know that you want what's best for the child, don't you?"

She stared at him another moment before sneering. "Then bring a doctor here. I'm not letting this baby out of my sight."

Another cry escaped from Cassidy, and she pressed her eyes closed.

Ty wanted to be next to her, to brush her hair out of her face and let her know everything was going to be okay.

But that wasn't an option right now.

He had to wait for the right opportunity.

"This baby is coming!" Cassidy yelled as her face squeezed with pain.

Jenn turned toward her.

When she did, Ty saw his opportunity.

It was now or never.

37

CASSIDY CHAMBERS

CASSIDY FELT THE BABY COMING.

He or she was almost here.

As a commotion sounded in the room, she jerked her eyes open.

Ty had tackled Jenn, and they wrestled beside her.

As Jenn let out a grunt and started to lunge at Ty, Cassidy grabbed the woman's hair. Cassidy pulled her back, surprising her just enough that Ty grabbed the gun in her hand.

He pointed it to the ceiling, where an accidental shot wouldn't hit anyone.

Jenn might be strong, but she wasn't stronger than her former Navy SEAL husband.

Ty wrenched the gun from her grip and handed it to Dillinger behind him.

As he flipped Jenn facedown and braced her wrists

behind her, Colton and Mac flooded into the room to take over.

Ty rushed toward Cassidy and pushed the damp strands of hair from her eyes. "You've got this." He readjusted the sheet, ensuring she was adequately covered.

Gratitude filled her until she felt like she might pass out. There was no time for that now. "I've never been so glad to see you."

"I can say the same." He quickly pressed a kiss on her lips. "Let's get this done."

"Ty . . ." Her voice trembled.

Their gazes caught. "I know you're scared. But we're going to get through this."

As Colton and Mac escorted Jenn from the room, she wrestled against them. "Let me go. I want my baby!"

Her shouts and curses were ignored. Her game was over.

Doc Clemson rushed inside as soon as the doorway was clear.

Suddenly, new fears replaced Cassidy's old ones.

What if her baby wasn't okay?

38

CASSIDY CHAMBERS

AN HOUR LATER, Cassidy was in the Lantern Beach Medical Clinic—and a healthy baby girl rested in her arms.

Despite the nightmare she'd been thrust into the middle of, everything had turned out okay.

Praise God.

Ty sat on the bed beside her, gazing at his baby girl. "It looks like we're going to have a merry Christmas after all."

A warm grin stretched across Cassidy's face. "Yes, we are."

Ty kissed the top of her head. "I was so worried about you."

"I was worried too. If you guys hadn't gotten there when you did . . ." Her voice broke, and she held her sleeping baby a little closer.

"The important thing is that we did—by the grace of God."

"You're right. That *is* the important thing. I hope Jenn receives the help she needs. Something isn't right with her, Ty."

"You can say that again. Apparently, from what Dillinger told me, she went off her meds about two weeks ago and disappeared. Her family has been searching for her, afraid she might do something dangerous."

"How did she end up in Lantern Beach of all places? Why here?"

"Apparently, she came to the island on vacation as a child. Her mom said she became obsessed with a family vacationing next door—a young couple with a baby. Jenn probably associated Lantern Beach with the perfect family life—the life she always wanted."

Cassidy frowned at the desperate images that filled her mind. "I know it might sound weird, but I actually feel bad for her."

"I do too."

Their gazes turned back to the perfect baby Cassidy held in her arms. Their daughter slept peacefully, clueless as to the trauma that had just happened.

"What should we name her?" Cassidy asked.

She and Ty had talked about it but hadn't come to any conclusions. They'd both decided that they would instinctively know after the baby was born what his or her name should be.

"I've been thinking about that a lot," Ty murmured as he stared at his daughter. "How about Faith?"

Cassidy smiled as his suggestion lingered in her mind. "I love that name."

"I was hoping you would."

"It's perfect for our daughter . . . for this situation. Faith is the only thing that's gotten us through. Time and time again, for that matter."

"You can say that again."

Cassidy glanced up at her husband and grinned. "I love you, Ty."

"I love you too, Cassidy." His gaze turned toward their daughter. "And you too, Faith Chambers."

"Merry Christmas to us."

Ty grinned. "Merry Christmas to us."

As they gazed at each other, music sounded in the distance. Ty rose from the bed and walked to the window. When he moved the curtain aside, Cassidy saw a group had gathered outside.

She scanned the familiar faces there. The guys from Blackout as well as the police station. Her Bible study group. Several people from church. Doc Clemson and Ernestine. Webster and Serena.

Carter Denver and his new wife, Sadie, stood at the front of the group, Carter with his guitar, as everyone else held candles and sang. "Oh, Come, All Ye Faithful" drifted through the air.

"What an appropriate song," Ty muttered.

"I'd say." Cassidy smiled.

The island's residents had showed her just how much they cared. And that was something Cassidy would never forget.

~~~

Thank you for reading *Silent Night*. If you enjoyed this book, please consider leaving a review.
~~~

ALSO BY CHRISTY BARRITT:

could lead to both her discovery and her demise. Can she bring justice to the island . . . or will the hidden currents surrounding her pull her under for good?

Flood Watch

The tide is high, and so is the danger on Lantern Beach. Still in hiding after infiltrating a dangerous gang, Cassidy Livingston just has to make it a few more months before she can testify at trial and resume her old life. But trouble keeps finding her, and Cassidy is pulled into a local investigation after a man mysteriously disappears from the island she now calls home. A recurring nightmare from her time undercover only muddies things, as does a visit from the parents of her handsome ex-Navy SEAL neighbor. When a friend's life is threatened, Cassidy must make choices that put her on the verge of blowing her cover. With a flood watch on her emotions and her life in a tangle, will Cassidy find the truth? Or will her past finally drown her?

Storm Surge

A storm is brewing hundreds of miles away, but its effects are devastating even from afar. Laid-back, loose, and light: that's Cassidy Livingston's new motto. But when a makeshift boat with a bloody cloth inside washes ashore near her oceanfront home, her detective instincts shift into gear . . . again. Seeking clues isn't the only thing on her mind—romance is heating up with next-door neighbor and former Navy SEAL Ty Chambers as well. Her heart wants the love and stability she's longed for her entire life. But her hidden identity only leads to a tidal wave of turbulence. As more answers emerge about the boat, the danger around her rises, creating a treacherous swell that threatens to reveal her past. Can Cassidy mind her own business, or will the storm surge of violence and corruption that has washed ashore on Lantern Beach leave her life in wreckage?

Dangerous Waters

Danger lurks on the horizon, leaving only two choices: find shelter or flee. Cassidy Livingston's new identity has begun to feel as comfortable as her favorite sweater. She's been tucked away on Lantern Beach for weeks, waiting to testify against a deadly gang, and is settling in to a new life she wants to last forever. When she thinks she spots someone malevolent from her past, panic swells inside her. If an enemy has found her, Cassidy won't be the only one who's a target. Everyone she's come to love will also be at risk. Dangerous waters threaten to pull her into an overpowering chasm she may never escape. Can Cassidy survive what lies ahead? Or has the tide fatally turned against her?

Perilous Riptide

Just when the current seems safer, an unseen danger emerges and threatens to destroy everything. When Cassidy Livingston finds a journal hidden deep in the recesses of her ice cream truck, her curiosity kicks into high gear. Islanders suspect that Elsa, the journal's owner, didn't die accidentally. Her final entry indicates their suspicions might be correct and that what Elsa observed on her final night may have led to her demise. Against the advice of Ty Chambers, her former Navy SEAL boyfriend, Cassidy taps into her detective skills and hunts for answers. But her search only leads to a skeletal body and trouble for both of them. As helplessness threatens to drown her, Cassidy is desperate to turn back time. Can Cassidy find what she needs to navigate the perilous situation? Or will the riptide surrounding her threaten everyone and everything Cassidy loves?

Deadly Undertow

The current's fatal pull is powerful, but so is one detective's will to live. When someone from Cassidy Livingston's past shows up on Lantern Beach and warns her of impending peril, opposing currents collide, threatening to drag her under. Running would be easy. But leaving would break her heart. Cassidy must decipher between the truth and lies, between reality and deception. Even more importantly, she must decide whom to trust and whom to fear. Her life depends on it. As danger rises and answers surface, everything Cassidy thought she knew is tested. In order to survive, Cassidy must take drastic measures and end the battle against the ruthless gang DH-7 once and for all. But if her final mission fails, the consequences will be as deadly as the raging undertow.

Tides of Deception

Change has come to Lantern Beach: a new police chief, a new season, and . . . a new romance? Austin Brooks has loved Skye Lavinia from the moment they met, but the walls she keeps around her seem impenetrable. Skye knows Austin is the best thing to ever happen to her. Yet she also knows that if he learns the truth about her past, he'd be a fool not to run. A chance encounter brings secrets bubbling to the surface, and danger soon follows. Are the life-threatening events plaguing them really accidents . . . or is someone trying to send a deadly message? With the tides on Lantern Beach come deception and lies. One question remains—who will be swept away as the water shifts? And will it bring the end for Austin and Skye, or merely the beginning?

Shadow of Intrigue

For her entire life, Lisa Garth has felt like a supporting character in the drama of life. The designation never bothered her—until now. Lantern Beach, where she's settled and runs a popular restaurant, has boarded up for the season. The slower pace leaves her with too much time alone. Braden Dillinger came to Lantern Beach to try to heal. The former Special Forces officer returned from battle with invisible scars and diminished hope. But his recovery is hampered by the fact that an unknown enemy is trying to kill him. From the moment Lisa and Braden meet, danger ignites around them, and both are drawn into a web of intrigue that turns their lives upside down. As shadows creep in, will Lisa and Braden be able to shine a light on the peril around them? Or will the encroaching darkness turn their worst nightmares into reality?

Storm of Doubt

A pastor who's lost faith in God. A romance writer who's lost faith in love. A faceless man with a deadly obsession. Nothing has felt right in Pastor Jack Wilson's world since his wife died two years ago. He hoped coming to Lantern Beach might help soothe the ragged edges of his soul. Instead, he feels more alone than ever. Novelist Juliette Grace came to the island to hide away. Though her professional life has never been better, her personal life has imploded. Her husband left her and a stalker's threats have grown more and more dangerous. When Jack saves Juliette from an attack, he sees the terror in her gaze and knows he must protect her. But when danger strikes again, will Jack be able to keep her safe? Or will the approaching storm prove too strong to withstand?

Winds of Danger

Wes O'Neill is perfectly content to hang with his friends and enjoy island life on Lantern Beach. Something begins to change inside him when Paige Henderson sweeps into his life. But the beautiful newcomer is hiding painful secrets beneath her cheerful facade. Police dispatcher Paige Henderson came to Lantern Beach riddled with guilt and uncertainties after the fallout of a bad relationship. When she meets Wes, she begins to open up to the possibility of love again. But there's something Wes isn't telling her—something that could change everything. As the winds shift, doubts seep into Paige's mind. Can Paige and Wes trust each other, even as the currents work against them? Or is trouble from the past too much to overcome?

Rains of Remorse

A stranger invades her home, leaving Rebecca Jarvis terrified. Above all, she must protect the baby growing inside her. Since her estranged husband died suspiciously six months earlier, Rebecca has been determined to depend on no one but herself. Her chivalrous new neighbor appears to be an answer to prayer. But who is Levi Stoneman really? Rebecca wants to believe he can help her, but she can't ignore her instincts. As danger closes in, both Rebecca and Levi must figure out whom they can trust. With Rebecca's baby coming soon, there's no time to waste. Can the truth prevail . . . or will remorse overpower the best of intentions?

Torrents of Fear

The woman lingering in the crowd can't be Allison . . . can she? Because Allison was pronounced dead six years ago. Musician Carter Denver knows only one person who's capable of helping him find answers: Sadie Thompson, his estranged best friend and someone who also knew Allison. He needs to know if he's losing his mind or if Allison could have survived her car accident. Could Allison really be alive? If so, why is she trying to harm Carter and Sadie? As the two try to find answers, can Sadie keep her feelings for Carter hidden? Could he ever care for her, or is the man of her dreams still in love with the woman now causing his nightmares?

On the Lookout

When Cassidy Chambers accepted the job as police chief on Lantern Beach, she knew the island had its secrets. But a suspicious death with potentially far-reaching implications will test all her skills—and threaten to reveal her true identity. Cassidy enlists the help of her husband, former Navy SEAL Ty Chambers. As they dig for answers, both uncover parts of their pasts that are best left buried. Not everything is as it seems, and they must figure out if their John Doe is connected to the secretive group that has moved onto the island. As facts materialize, danger on the island grows. Can Cassidy and Ty discover the truth about the shadowy crimes in their cozy community? Or has darkness permanently invaded their beloved Lantern Beach?

Attempt to Locate

A fun girls' night out turns into a nightmare when armed robbers barge into the store where Cassidy and her friends are shopping. As the situation escalates and the men escape, a massive manhunt launches on Lantern Beach to apprehend the dangerous trio. In the midst of the chaos, a potential foe asks for Cassidy's help. He needs to find his sister who fled from the secretive Gilead's Cove community on the island. But the more Cassidy learns about the seemingly untouchable group, the more her unease grows. The pressure to solve both cases continues to mount. But as the gravity of the situation rises, so does the danger. Cassidy is determined to protect the island and break up the cult . . . but doing so might cost her everything.

First Degree Murder

Police Chief Cassidy Chambers longs for a break from the recent crimes plaguing Lantern Beach. She simply wants to enjoy her friends' upcoming wedding, to prepare for the busy tourist season about to slam the island, and to gather all the dirt she can on the suspicious community that's invaded the town. But trouble explodes on the island, sending residents—including Cassidy—into a squall of uneasiness. Cassidy may have more than one enemy plotting her demise, and the collateral damage seems unthinkable. As the temperature rises, so does the pressure to find answers. Someone is determined that Lantern Beach would be better off without their new police chief. And for Cassidy, one wrong move could mean certain death.

Dead on Arrival

With a highly charged local election consuming the community, Police Chief Cassidy Chambers braces herself for a challenging day of breaking up petty conflicts and tamping down high emotions. But when widespread food poisoning spreads among potential voters across the island, Cassidy smells something rotten in the air. As Cassidy examines every possibility to uncover what's going on, local enigma Anthony Gilead again comes on her radar. The man is running for mayor and his cult-like following is growing at an alarming rate. Cassidy feels certain he has a spy embedded in her inner circle. The problem is that her pool of suspects gets deeper every day. Can Cassidy get to the bottom of what's eating away at her peaceful island home? Will voters turn out despite the outbreak of illness plaguing their tranquil town? And the even bigger question: Has darkness come to stay on Lantern Beach?

Plan of Action

A missing Navy SEAL. Danger at the boiling point. The ultimate showdown. When Police Chief Cassidy Chambers' husband, Ty, disappears, her world is turned upside down. His truck is discovered with blood inside, crashed in a ditch on Lantern Beach, but he's nowhere to be found. As they launch a manhunt to find him, Cassidy discovers that someone on the island has a deadly obsession with Ty. Meanwhile, Gilead's Cove seems to be imploding. As danger heightens, federal law enforcement officials are called in. The cult's growing threat could lead to the pinnacle standoff of good versus evil. A clear plan of action is needed or the results will be devastating. Will Cassidy find Ty in time, or will she face a gut-wrenching loss? Will Anthony Gilead finally be unmasked for who he really is and be brought to justice? Hundreds of innocent lives are at stake . . . and not everyone will come out alive.

LANTERN BEACH BLACKOUT

Dark Water

Colton Locke can't forget the black op that went terribly wrong. Desperate for a new start, he moves to Lantern Beach, North Carolina, and forms Blackout, a private security firm. Despite his hero status, he can't erase the mistakes he's made. For the past year, Elise Oliver hasn't been able to shake the feeling that there's more to her husband's death than she was told. When she finds a hidden box of his personal possessions, more questions—and suspicions—arise. The only person she trusts to help her is her husband's best friend, Colton Locke. Someone wants Elise dead. Is it because she knows too much? Or is it to keep her from finding the truth? The Blackout team must uncover dark secrets hiding beneath seemingly still waters. But those very secrets might just tear the team apart.

Safe Harbor

Guilt over past mistakes haunts former Navy

SEAL Dez Rodriguez. When he's asked to guard a pop star during a music festival on Lantern Beach, he's all set for what he hopes is a breezy assignment. Bree hasn't found fame to be nearly as fulfilling as she dreamed. Instead, she's more like a carefully crafted character living out a pre-scripted story. When a stalker's threats become deadly, her life—and career—are turned upside down. From the start, Bree sees her temporary bodyguard as a player, and Dez sees Bree as a spoiled rich girl. But when they're thrown together in a fight for survival, both must learn to trust. Can Dez protect Bree—and his carefully guarded heart? Or will their safe harbor ultimately become their death trap?

Ripple Effect

Griff McIntyre never expected his ex-wife and three-year-old daughter to come to Lantern Beach. After an abduction attempt, they're desperate for safety. Now Griff's not letting either of them out of his sight. Bethany knows Griff is the only one who can protect them, despite the fact that he broke her heart. But she'll do anything to keep her daughter safe—even if it means playing nicely with a man she can't stand. As peril ripples through their lives, Griff and Bethany must work together to protect their daughter. But an unseen enemy wants something from them . . . and will stop at nothing to get it. When disaster strikes, can Griff keep his family safe? Or will past mistakes bring the ultimate failure?

Rising Tide

Benjamin James knows there's a traitor within his former command. The rest of his team might even think it's him. As danger closes in, he must clear himself and stop a deadly plot by a dangerous terrorist group. All CJ Compton wanted was a new start after her career ended under suspicion. Working as the house manager for private security group Blackout seems perfect. But there's more trouble here than what she left behind. As the tide rushes in, the stakes continue to rise. If the Blackout team fails, it's not just Lantern Beach at stake—it's the whole country. Can Benjamin and CJ overcome their differences and work together to find the truth?

LANTERN BEACH BLACKOUT: THE NEW RECRUITS

Rocco

Former Navy SEAL and new Blackout recruit Rocco Foster is on a simple in and out mission. But the operation turns complicated when an unsuspecting woman wanders into the line of fire. Peyton Ellison's life mission is to sprinkle happiness on those around her. When a cupcake delivery turns into a fight for survival, she must trust her rescuer—a handsome stranger—to keep her safe. Rocco is determined to figure out why someone is targeting Peyton. First, he must keep the intriguing woman safe and earn her trust. But threats continue to pummel them as incriminating evidence emerges and pits them against each other. With time running out, the two must set aside both their growing attraction and their doubts about each other in order to work together. But the perilous facts they discover leave them wondering what exactly the truth is . . . and if the truth can be trusted.

Axel

Women are missing. Private security firm Blackout must find them before another victim disappears. Axel Hendrix likes to live on the edge. That's why being a Navy SEAL suited him so well. But after his last mission, he cut his losses and joined Blackout instead. His team's latest case involves an undercover investigation on Lantern Beach. Olivia Rollins came to the island to escape her problems—and danger. When trouble from her past shows up in town, she impulsively blurts she's engaged to Axel, the womanizing man she's seen while waitressing. Now, she may not be the only one in danger. So could Axel. Axel knows Olivia might be his chance to find answers and that acting like her fiancé is the perfect cover for his latest assignment. But he doesn't like throwing Olivia into the middle of such a dangerous situation. Nor is he comfortable with the feelings she stirs inside him. With Olivia's life—as well as both their hearts—on the line, Axel must uncover the truth and stop an evil plan before more lives are destroyed.

Beckett

When the daughter of a federal judge is abducted, private security firm Blackout must find her. Psychologist Samantha Reynolds doesn't know why someone is targeting her. Even after a risky mission to save her, danger still lingers. She's determined to use her insights into the human mind to help decode the deadly clues being left in the wake of her rescue. Former Navy SEAL Beckett Jones needs to figure out who's responsible for the crimes hounding Sami. He's not sure why he's so protective of the woman he rescued, but he'll do anything to keep her safe—even if it means risking his heart. As the body count rises, there's no room for error. Beckett and Sami must both tear down the careful walls they've built around themselves in order to survive. If they don't figure out who's responsible, the madman will continue his death spree ... and one of them might be next.

Gabe

When former Navy SEAL and current Blackout operative Gabe Michaels is almost killed in a hit-and-run, the aftermath completely upends his life. He's no longer safe—and he's not the only one. Dr. Autumn Spenser came to Lantern Beach to start fresh. But while treating Gabe after his accident, she senses there's more to what happened to him than meets the eye. When she digs deeper into his past, she never expects to be drawn into a deadly dilemma. Gabe has been infatuated with the pretty doctor since the day they met. Now, can he keep her from harm? Could someone out of his league ever return his feelings or will her past hurts keep them apart? As danger continues to pummel them, Gabe and Autumn are thrown together in a quest to find answers. More important than their growing attraction, they must stay alive long enough to stop the person desperate to destroy them.

ABOUT THE AUTHOR

USA Today has called Christy Barritt's books "scary, funny, passionate, and quirky."

Christy writes both mystery and romantic suspense novels that are clean with underlying messages of faith. Her books have won the Daphne du Maurier Award for Excellence in Suspense and Mystery, have been twice nominated for the Romantic Times Reviewers' Choice Award, and have finaled for both a Carol Award and Foreword Magazine's Book of the Year.

She is married to her Prince Charming, a man who thinks she's hilarious—but only when she's not trying to be. Christy is a self-proclaimed klutz, an avid music lover who's known for spontaneously bursting into song, and a road trip aficionado.

When she's not working or spending time with her family, she enjoys singing, playing the guitar, and exploring small, unsuspecting towns where people have no idea how accident-prone she is.

Find Christy online at:
www.christybarritt.com
www.facebook.com/christybarritt
www.twitter.com/cbarritt

Sign up for Christy's newsletter to get information on all of her latest releases here: www.christybarritt.com/newsletter-sign-up/

If you enjoyed this book, please consider leaving a review.